STARTING OVER

LUCIFER'S BREED MC
BOOK 3

BY RYDER DANE

ISBN-10# 1-945012-17-X
ISBN-13# 978-1-945012-17-4

Edited by Vinvatar Publishing

Artwork by Jess Buffett Graphic Designs

Published by Vinvatar Publishing
Website: Vinvatar.com

TABLE OF CONTENTS

PROLOGUE

She finished spreading her brother's ashes in the Missouri river. The tall, wide shouldered, hard as nails man she'd known was now gone, and in her heart was the biggest void she'd never wanted to imagine. Tuck wouldn't be there when she fucked up, or became cornered by some well meaning bastard that wanted to change the Dyke's sexual orientation. She was on her own now, and she was still feeling the rage at God for allowing the only one in the world she loved to be murdered by a damned bunch of killers that even the cops were afraid to pull over on the highway.

As a toddler, her parents and brother had spoiled her. She'd grown into a snaggle toothed, first grade princess when Tuck came to school to pick her up early one day. She'd never seen her parents alive after that horrible day. The official cause of death was a gas explosion in the house. Tuck had been blown out of the backdoor or he wouldn't have lived to be there to pick her up to tell her that mommy and daddy were dead, and with the angels now. He had been barely eighteen years old himself, could have left her for the state to take, but he didn't do that. He took her and left the area that day.

It wasn't until she was eight that she heard Tuck telling the man he worked for that their parents had been killed by a man that their father was going to testify against. Mr. McCormick was an older gentleman that owned a bar in the middle of nowhere, outside of a little town called Betwixt. There wasn't much to the town: a post office, a general store, two gas stations, and a diner. Mr. McCormick helped Tuck claim the insurance money from the house, and their father's life insurance policy. At eighteen and scared of his shadow, Tuck hadn't even thought about such things as insurance claims. At the time, all he was thinking was to get his little sister, and get the hell away from the killer.

Tuck had seen the men that had killed their parents, and when she'd turned twenty one, he began his hunt for the bastards. She'd heard from him from time to time, and even wrote things down he told her to remember for him, like names and numbers. Once in a while he would mention a few men that he liked, but increasingly in the past few months, his calls were fewer and farther between.

From the day she began sprouting breasts, she was in disguise. Her hair was as short as she could cut it, and she wore nothing but boys clothing at all times. Makeup had never touched her smooth cheeks or eyes, and the only lipstick she could claim to have used was lip balm. The bar patrons knew that she was a girl, there was no hiding her curves or her voice. Letting them believe that she was more boy than girl was the only protection she was able to use from amorous rough necks, farmers, and drifters. Other than the knives she kept in her engineer boots, and the 1911 style semi auto Colt she carried when she was away from the bar. Her plain appearance was her best asset.

She hadn't gone to school, Tuck and the old man had taught her Math, English, and Science, to the best of their limited abilities. They lived so far outside of any town with a school that she would have been home schooled anyway.

The old man had passed away three months ago. He hadn't told her that he had prostate cancer until he was too weak to get out of bed one day. She knew he wasn't feeling well, and had taken him to his Doctor every other week or so for quite some time now. She got him into the old Studebaker truck he loved so much and driven the eighty miles to the hospital. He hadn't been back home two days before she found him dead in his room. He'd taken the entire bottle of pain medication, washed down with a bottle of whiskey.

His funeral had been the biggest one of the year for the local funeral home. There must've been twenty people at the graveside to pray his soul into heaven. She had shared hugs and handshakes with most of the attendees, but she was too numb to celebrate his life. All that she could think of at the time is that she was alone.

She had been named the sole heir in the old man's will. It was a surprise to her that he hadn't included Tuck to at least inherit the bar, but there was no one left for her to ask why.

Last week, she'd gotten an anonymous phone call telling her to pick up Tuck. It was dark and raining by the time she got to Lindell. She drove up to a deserted garage, and put the truck in park. A black van pulled in behind her and two men got out of the van. They went to the back and she could see them carrying what appeared to be a body, wrapped in plastic bags. Their burden was heaved into the bed of her truck, and the men got back into the van and left. Once they were out of sight, she jumped from the truck and ran to the open tailgate, climbing into the bed. She took the knife from her boot and sliced the plastic from boots to his neck, crying all the while. She pulled the plastic from his head and lost her mind in those few seconds it took for her to recognize her brother's face in the light from her Maglite. She'd known when she answered the phone, but had hoped that it would turn out to be a mistake.

The police had no leads, or so they said anyway. She knew who Tuck's killer was from the research she had done and was continuing to do, she knew that the man was the same one that had murdered her parents.

Her plan was not solid yet, but the son-of-a-bitch would pay, and she would bathe in his blood if she got the chance. She had a few things to do first, and if there was one thing she was good at, it was planning. She had some skills to perfect, and a few arrangements to make. Once she was gone, she didn't plan on returning, but one never knew what life or death would bring about. "Hope for the best, but expect the worst."

CHAPTER 1

Eighteen months later:

War was frustrated. He was disgusted by the shit and politics that came with being a show horse. Wolfman had pulled five of the Club's Presidents into his own entourage as additional bodyguards. He was expected to be at the fucker's beck and call anytime day or night. He knew Wolfman was planning something, and it wouldn't be beneficial to the five men he'd pulled rank on either.

He was playing poker with Fetch and Joey when Slick pulled a wooden bench to their table and sat down. He at least waited until they'd finished their hand before he started running his mouth.

"I ain't saying we got a rat here, but someone poisoned Opie, we found him an hour ago. Fucker's still foaming at the mouth, he's been dead for a while." He looked around the room before turning back to the three at the table. He leaned in closer, "Sea is missing, and Aaron is all fucked up. He got the same shit Opie got, he's opening and closing his mouth, but nothing is coming out. The shit he drank was like drain cleaner." He sat back a little still looking around the room. "Someone firebombed the shed, the cops just told the guys at the door, and Wolfman is looking like he's gonna pop a vein."

War didn't believe that this was all Slick wanted to say, he was here at this table for a reason. "What in the hell is going on? Last I heard we weren't at war. I can see why someone would want to take Aaron out, not the rest." He kept a stern lock on his face, even if he wanted to laugh. Opie was Slick's best friend, but something just wasn't right here with the way Slick told them about the tragedies. "Who forced them to drink the stuff?" He wasn't supposed to know about the shed, it was actually a small pole barn where Wolfman's slaves were manufacturing Meth. More than likely it blew up rather than was firebombed.

"Wolfman is nervous. He thinks he's next and he is pretending to be too sick to come out of his rooms. Look man, I don't know what's going on here, alright? All I know is that Opey is dead, Aaron is dying, and Sea is missing. Our president is hiding like a fuckin' rabbit up in his room, leaving the rest of us here with our thumbs in our asses wondering whose next, and who the enemy is. There are fifty of us here, and unless Sea walks through that door soon, I'm gonna say we got forty-nine people now."

Fetch was one of Wolfman's trusted minions, just like Slick was, but he never flinched at the news. He was staring at War, and stood up.

"You might want to sit down before I misunderstand your aggressive act here, Fetch. I haven't left this fucking building for three days. Joey here hasn't either. So sit back down before I decide you're asking me to dance."

"I gotta take a piss, don't get your shit all stirred. I know you've been here, no one's making accusations." He turned his back and walked away. War and Joey turned back to Slick.

"Cut the shit Slick, just come out with what Wolfy wants us to know and you can go back and tell him whatever the fuck you want to tell the man. If he's hiding out, then the members will start to notice, and while the man might be pickled and fuckin' smoked most of the time, he ain't dumb." Joey had a way with words, and he was one of the few men that War could actually tolerate in this place. He nodded his head in agreement as they both looked at Slick.

"I'm not the stooge you two assholes think I am. Fetch ain't either. Two days ago Wolfman got a letter. You know how important he thinks he is, he's too important to read his mail and always has Zero read it to him. Usually its bill collectors and shit like that. This was a real letter. It said that bad things would be happening if he didn't put a gun to his head and blow his fuckin' brains out in the middle of town, under the caution light. He thinks it's one of the former presidents trying to cause shit, but me and Fetch, we talked, and we think it's personal, ya know? Wolf has pissed off a lot of people."

That got their attention. Joey sneered as he asked, "So what are we supposed to do? If someone has a legit grudge, I can't see a problem with Wolfy taking care of it in his usual way. He has me sitting here on my ass or standing at his back, as many people as he's pissed off, do you even know how many or who they are?"

The men played another hand, dealing Slick in, and he didn't bother to try to cheat this time. Everyone knew he cheated in a normal game, but too many were afraid of his closeness to the Prez, Wolfman, to call him on it.

No one had enough information to decide where to look for the person killing off the brothers, but each man had his own thoughts. War held his ideas close to his chest. If there had been three men who deserved killing, yeah, the guy picked some good candidates. He glanced around the room, keeping his eyes moving even when he saw someone that he knew mostly by reputation. It wouldn't be good if Slick saw him looking at any one person for longer than a second, he would try to find a connection. They didn't call the man Slick for nothing, he was everything his tag implied.

The skank sucking Race off, was one of those women with no gag reflex and the ability to vacuum the cum from a man's prick in five minutes or less. They called her Dew Drop, but War hadn't indulged her taste for a man's cum. He liked a good blow job as much as the next man, but ol' Dew Drop was showing signs of wear quick, and the needle marks on her inner elbows were a big problem for him. He preferred Gummi, at least she didn't scrape his cock with jagged teeth and a mouthful of sores. She didn't deep throat a man voluntarily, but she worked that tongue of hers around a cock while it was buried into the back of her throat. He felt sorry for the woman, but she wanted to belong to the club, and she was tougher than she looked. Someone had long ago abused her, and either knocked out her teeth or pulled them out, she was also missing an eye. Since the first night he'd woken up with her lips wrapped around his dick, she'd been his favorite.

Elton was pounding his meat into some female that made the mistake of letting them tie her to a tabletop, and she would be a messed up zombie by morning. She'd already had at least five guys fucking her holes, and Elton was just another in line.

Slick twitched and put his cards face down on the table before reaching into his shirt pocket and answering a call. "Yeah, I got it, where? Thanks, man." He put the phone back in his pocket and shook his head, "forty nine confirmed. That was Donnie, the cop. Sea was found in the alley behind Double D's, dead." He picked up his cards and the game continued.

*****

She had been trying her best to find a way to get to him when the solution presented itself in a left side of the problem kind of way. If you can't get to the snake, you destroy his habitat, he'll either move on, or slither out of his hole and try to fight to keep his territory.

She'd opted for destruction of habitat. It shouldn't have surprised her that she was not the only one that hated the Breed's president. Maisie, her newfound friend, well she was going the more direct route, genocide.

River had driven into town and taken a room at the local weekly rental place. It was a nice hotel in the fifties, now it was a place for anyone who had cash to pay up front for a room on a weekly basis. Prostitutes and druggies lived there, a few single moms who had no other options, but there were a few people like her, just renting a room until they could find a more permanent place to sleep.

There had been no problem getting a job at Double D's, she could toss a bottle and draw a draft beer with minimal head as easily as she could breathe, and the owner of the place was eager to hire a bartender slash barmaid that had her skills.

Now she was established in the area. Her plans were right on track, until last night at least. She'd just come back from torching an old metal building that housed the biker's meth lab, and stumbled upon a woman that was even shorter than herself, trying to heave a big body onto a tarp behind the sandwich shop.

The little woman had been startled by the way River ran up to her, almost falling over the legs of the dead guy. She'd looked down just in time to stop herself from meeting the concrete in a personal way, and saw the girl cowering against the wall of the building. The dead guy was foaming at the mouth and it was obvious that the girl had a hand in his killing. Seeing the vest he wore, or his cut, as the bikers called it, made her smile and she decided to help the little woman if she could.

Gummi was the girl's name at the clubhouse, but she told River about her life before Wolfman had taken her from her home in Arkansas. The bikers had been riding through town while she had been walking home from a basketball game where she'd ditched her date. She was bitter and River couldn't blame her. Wolfman had stopped the entire club just long enough to snag her from the sidewalk. He'd knocked her out, and she had no idea how she'd ended up at their campsite the next morning. Her real name was Maisie Jean Lassiter, and she was now twenty-eight. As she said, "There ain't nuthin' for me to go back to. I tried calling my mother, but she went all ape shit on me and told me I was dead, and to leave her alone."

It seemed a bit strange, talking about the little woman's history while they rolled Sea onto a blue plastic tarp. Stranger still, while they tugged and dragged their heavy load the hundred feet or so to rest it near the grease box where the grill kitchen dumped vats of used frying oil and lard. Gummi was an evil genius, and River planned to assist her in her endeavors to a point.

She dropped Gummi off on the road about a hundred feet from the driveway that led to the MC's home base. The woman disappeared into the trees, and River kept driving past the dirt two track just like any other vehicle would do, but she was scoping out places that might give a person a bit of cover. She needed some idea of who came and went on a daily basis, then she could plan her timing better. With Gummi's assistance, even if she wasn't aware of helping her, she would have eyes and ears inside of the club itself. Befriending the girl hadn't been a bad decision, in fact, it was as if fate herself had handed River what she needed to accomplish her ultimate goal.

CHAPTER 2

Wolfman stayed holed up in his rooms for four days before he showed his face in the bar. Fetch and Slick stayed at his side while he was walking around, acting like he was the bad motherfucker that he had always been. Only the way his eyes tracked the room and rested on potential assassins, showed his concern. Right now his gaze was trained on War, and Race wondered what would come of that suspicion.

War might be well liked and respected by the club's members, but Race had his own plans for being Wolfman's replacement, and it might be time for him to have a discussion with the man. War had to know that it was past time for Wolfy to go to pasture, but the fucker wouldn't leave his post voluntarily. He got a nut every time he looked in the mirror because of his importance.

Race could identify with that position at least that was the plan. He wanted the entire club to get out of the pharmaceutical business. He had no problem with a bit of weed, but that other shit was just fucking too many people up. He didn't really give a shit what adults did to their bodies, kids were entirely different. Kids were being dumbed down enough without providing them with poison. His own cousin had gotten into some of the shit and ran into the middle of a four-way in Dallas during rush hour. He hopped on the hood of a car, the driver slammed on his brakes and Cory flew off the car, landing in the path of a metro bus. That had been a fucking circus, and no one came out feeling at peace after the funeral. Yeah, Meth would be a big problem with him once he took over the president's post.

He'd been to every MC chapter that claimed membership status, and even visited some of the affiliates over the past two years. There was a lot of opposition to the way Wolfman was taking the club. Between the heat and the rival groups, not to mention the drug lords from down in South America taking over territory from the small basically harmless bike clubs, and the infighting between the older established clubs, something had to be decided soon. It was time to modernize the Breed, or they would be a moldering blurb in history books.

The explosion that rocked the building had everyone hitting the deck. Ceiling tiles and rock lath flew through the room, and Race caught a sharp piece of shingle on his cheek. Electrical wires arced and a few moans could be heard. The old rotted timber that supported the roof was burning, and shit was still falling on the men inside of the building. A secondary explosion caused the occupants to head for the exits. Some of the men had guns drawn in case this ambush came complete with snipers stationed to take them out one by one.

The crowd of bikers that could do nothing but stare at the smoldering pile of iron and melted tires, was kept at bay because the tanks kept exploding. That explained the secondary explosion they'd heard. Men were doing their best to hose the burning bikes and ignoring the building, until the fire caught the gas lines. The explosion from that had several men running toward the five-hundred-gallon propane tank beside the building to shut the gas off before that tank exploded too.

They were too late, the sidewall had fallen over and the flames that danced along the painted wood burned a deeper blue. Both Race and War stopped and immediately reversed their tracks. They were shouting, trying to warn the men in front of the burning building. "Get down, run, and get the fuck away from the building!" Was shouted and "Bomb!" was the only word that finally got most of their attention. Fetch, Slick, and Zero, were standing with Wolfman talking. War really hated to save the fuckers, and from the way Race seemed to hesitate too they exchanged a long look and each man turned aside to start grabbing men by the arm and yelling at them to get down, run and "Move your asses!"

Race saw the whores and club's passarounds standing behind the fire, they were all staring and not moving, unaware of the danger. "Fuckin' women." He started towards them, yelling at them to "get the fuck away from the fire." He tackled three of them, and they screamed, but he told them to "shut the fuck up." Gummi was still standing, ignoring his demand that she "hit the dirt, you dumb Bitch."

War came up on her left side, and tackled her to the ground. "You women crawl your asses behind the trailers, if you want to live to see another day! That propane tank is going to blow and it will be like the fires of hell hitting your skin. Move it."

Billy, Pete, Mambo and two other men he knew only by sight, were leading the females away. Gummi turned to look at him with her one eye and smiled. War watched her jerk her head to the side at him, "you should leave now." She raised her hand, and he could see that she held a small, cheap cell phone. Her finger sat on a key, and he understood exactly what was going on.

Okay, this was unexpected. He nodded at her and said, "Let's do this, give me a second to stand up, and I'll get us to safety. When I say "now", push the key, and be ready to go."

She looked puzzled, but nodded her head. He looked around them and saw no one was paying any attention to them, good. He stood, and hauled her over his shoulder beginning to run. "Now," and he imagined her finger touching off the detonation. It wouldn't have mattered if he or Race had gotten to the tank to shut it off. The tank must've been rigged before the first explosion, and as his boots ate up the dusty ground with the woman hanging over his shoulder, he counted the seconds.

He could see that Race and the rest of the men had kept the women moving instead of allowing them to take cover behind the fragile metal trailers, and headed their way. The explosion behind them rolled the trailers, jerking them from the metal tie downs and cement blocks. Screams and men with burning clothing could be seen and heard from the distance that the small party of survivors stood. The propane tank fell from the sky in pieces and landed on men and iron.

Sirens could be heard in the distance, and War held Gummi until she stopped shaking. "Are you alright?" Her nod was jerky, but physically he knew there wasn't a scratch on her. Her mental state, well, that was another thing. She kept watching the flames and naming the men she recognized still standing by the light of the burning pile of rubble.

"You don't say anything to anybody, do you hear me? The place was a nest of vipers and depraved motherfuckers, and you did what no one else had the guts to do. Just shut it, and look like you're scared." War lectured.

He sent her to sit with her friends, and walked towards the burning pile of what used to be the National headquarters of Lucifer's Breed MC, Bracket Hills, Ohio. Race walked beside him. "What the fuck just happened here?" He shook his head and kept going. He wasn't certain why, but he was sure that Gummi wasn't working alone.

The screams of pain and fright coming from under the rubble made every survivor shiver. Those men and women, who'd been sleeping or fucking in the basement rooms, were trapped with nowhere to go, and from the amount of choking smoke, no way out alive.

Wolfman was barely alive, and Race knew that the man wouldn't last long, so he left the silently screaming corpse lying with his three favorite henchmen who were incinerated into ashes. They hadn't moved when Race and War shouted their warnings, and they'd paid the price. There might be enough of them to identify by DNA samples, but the men left standing agreed that their own stupidity and arrogance had gotten them killed.

The hurried head count including the injured, told them that fourteen men were dead, or missing. Ten men were badly burned, and two of those would pray for death when the pain over rode the endorphins. The remaining men stood shell shocked to see the burning pile of rubble that had been the National Headquarters for the Breed since the club started.

The fire trucks rushed through the gate and set up camp, but by then, the damage had been done, there were no more screams or human noises coming from beneath the burning pile. There were cops everywhere, every agency in the state was represented within the first five hours, and if Race guessed right, there was a Fed or two there as well.

There wasn't a bike that had been saved from the mess, including Race's stripped down Indian Chief. It was an older model, but still a classic, and he was pissed about the waste of a beautiful machine. War was cussing a blue streak when he tried to touch the handlebars of his Chopper, and Race could relate to the man's outrage.

They all stood in the warm sunshine and waited to be grilled by the various agents and detectives. No one knew anything, and the women were almost given a free pass. Gummi was one that was given more pitiful looks than demands for answers, and she glanced at War with a small smile.

Race began organizing the bikers as soon as they were let go from the interrogations, and emergency shelters were found. Luckily several of the members lived in houses in town and in the rural area surrounding the town, so many of them found places to sleep that night. A couple of travel trailers and a pop-up tent camper sat out of the perimeter of the fire scene, and both Race and War set up a command post in the pop-up. Neither man wanted to relinquish any ground to the other.

The second day of hearing themselves speaking the same words at the same time made them aware that there had to be a better way to rebuild the Breed. Two Bosses wouldn't cut it, and there hadn't even been a hasty vote to decide who would temporarily lead them until the National vote happened.

They were eating dinner at Double D's when War decided that they needed to talk, and the little barmaid with the chin length hair and beautiful blue eyes was summoned to bring a pitcher, two glasses and four shots of Jack. "Darlin', tell the bartender that if he tries to substitute the Jack for that rotgut shit he tried to give me yesterday, I'll pull his nuts off and hand them to you." She nodded and grinned, before turning away to get their order.

He eyed Race, who was eyeing him. "We need to talk, and I don't see any other way around it. The suits will be at the property in the morning, and we will need to have a plan before they get there. I have a plan, if you don't like it say so, and I'll listen to your ideas. Fair enough?"

He got the nod from the other man, and waited to continue until the curvy little gal had poured them each a beer from the pitcher and set two shots next to the glasses. "Is there anything else I can get for you boys?" The tandem "No" answered her question and she burst out laughing.

The men shared only their hair color in looks, reddish brown, while one had brown eyes, the other had blue. The one with the blue eyes had a scruffy looking beard, and the other one had a sculpted beard. Both were handsome enough to make a girl drench her panties if she was wearing any, and their size was a pretty even match. She was not immune to their appeal, but she didn't want to get tangled up with a biker. She would be leaving town soon, and going back to her life in the betwixt and between of Kansas and Missouri. Her mission here had been accomplished, even if she hadn't personally dealt the death blows. From what she'd gleaned from the bikers that came in and the cops that frequented the place, Wolfman and his favorite henchmen were dead, incinerated by a gas explosion. She was still smiling when she went back to the bar and began cleaning out the service tubs that had accumulated during the dinner hours.

Race was doing his share of watching the plump cheeks of her ass sway away from their table and knew that War was watching just as avidly as he was. He poured the first shot down his throat and swallowed the beer in his glass, while War did the same.

War started talking. "Okay, this is the way I see it. Both of us are capable of running the Club, no dispute there. Both of us obviously want the club to be steered in different directions from the old ways, because we think going legit in several areas will be beneficial to the Club. The one thing we don't seem to agree on is that I am no threat to you becoming the Prez. I don't particularly want the spotlight, and I don't want the headache. I'm used to being a chapter Prez and now I'm in limbo. There's a new leader back home and he's doing a great job. I can go home, but there isn't anyone waiting for me and seeing as how you'll need help, I'll settle for being the VP. If you have someone else in mind for the job, talk to me, if you don't think we can work together, tell me now, I get up, I walk away, and I start campaigning. I'm not good at taking orders, so I'm without options unless I want to be a fuckin' grunt." He shook his head. He hoped Race would agree to the terms he'd set, if not, this was going to be a bloody fight outside and inside the MC Group. War would have the southern chapter's votes, and Race would probably sway the Northern vote.

Both men wouldn't hesitate to play dirty, no matter if they did, they would probably be playing the same tricks on each other. This synced thought thing or whatever it was called, was a pain in the ass. It was uncanny how much the men thought alike.

The offer was better than he'd hoped for, if they presented a united front, any opposition to their reign would be squashed. Race nodded thoughtfully. "Why? You and I are pretty evenly matched. Why are you so willing to take second place when the grand prize is up for grabs?" He didn't like the look that came over War's face.

"You want to know why? Well, I guess I should tell you, a warning such as it is. You fucking start taking the Breed down the same shitty drugged out road that Wolfman did, I'll be right there to drop your ass where you stand. The job goes to your head, and I will be there to either knock some sense into it, or cut it off at the neck. Checks and balances are needed man, the same as any corporation that's well organized. The club goes more modern and run like a business in the National level, the Chapters gain respect and learn by the example we project."

Race found himself liking War, even if the man had just threatened to beat his ass or kill him, whichever he figured the situation called for. It was fair enough as far as he was concerned. They wanted the same results, for Lucifer's Breed to become united and still continue to live as free people without fighting and fucking with selling and manufacturing drugs.

"Okay, say I bite, I take the bait. Remember something yourself, I don't fear you, and if you get too fucking proud of your position, and start shit that tarnishes that position, *you* will be the one with me at your back ready to do what needs to be done. You got that?"

In answer, War poured their glasses full and raised the remaining shot glass, Race raised his, and they shot the whiskey, and drained their glasses of beer. They left when the pitcher was empty, and River found two twenty dollar tips on the table when she went to clean it off.

CHAPTER 3

Now that her goal had been realized, it was time for her to leave the area. She wondered what Maisie would do now that the men who'd hurt her and taken her life away were dead. The entire deal was wacked as far as she could tell. She wished her little comrade well, but it wasn't likely the woman would leave. She had nowhere to go now, and from what River understood, she had very little money to live off of to begin with.

She walked into the bar and grill the next day and saw the owner's wife, Dena, trying to mop the scarred wooden floors on her hands and knees. The woman was past sixty, yet here she was scrubbing the floor as if her life depended on it. River bent down to get the old girl's attention and saw such misery on the woman's face that she took the brush from her fragile hand and raised them both up to their feet. She held her in a tight embrace and the woman let loose her grief.

Five minutes of cries and sobs had soaked her shirt, but she held the woman until the worst of the storm had passed, before asking, "What happened?"

"Darnell had a severe stroke last night, and he almost died. He's paralyzed on his entire right side, and I'm scared." Dena sniffed, and drew away from River. "I don't know how to run the bar, and if they let him come home at all, I'll have to be with him."

Well hell, how could she abandon the nice, old woman now? She had come in early today to give

Darnell her two week's notice, and she knew as certain as the sun would shine that she would stay on and help.

*****

Three months later:

The bikers were throwing a party, and she was bringing the housewarming gift from Double D's.

In the past weeks she had taken over managing the bar and she had actually enjoyed herself changing things up. The music was a good mix of old and new, and she had hired Maisie to work as the kitchen assistant. The girl now had a set of brand new teeth that she showed off every time she could find a reason to smile. She had also moved out of the trailers that the bikers had set up until they relocated into the old winery almost directly across from where the old clubhouse had been located. Today was the day that the little woman had worn her new prosthetic eye to fill in the space that had been vacant for so long, and she looked beautiful in River's opinion. More importantly, Maisie felt beautiful. She'd cried once the eye was in place, and only stopped thanking River once she'd been told to shut it.

"You've more than earned it, my friend. I love the hair too. Stella did a great job streaking it with that beautiful shade of blue."

Maisie was at the bar today supervising the cleaning and making sure that the crew that they'd hired to clean the exhaust blowers and kitchen ceiling didn't help themselves to the liquor or anything else. Since she'd come to work for Double D's, she avoided the Breed members' like the plague. She mostly hid out in the kitchen when one of the Brothers' showed up, River understood and let her get away with it.

The housewarming gift was a case of whiskey and a keg of beer, five gallons of potato salad, and thirty loaves of bread for the barbequed meat that Kink had told her the club was providing for their guests. The best part of the giving was that the bar's logo was on the stickers that she'd put on everything she was bringing. It was good promotion for the bar, and tax deductible as advertising. The Breed were good customers and she planned to keep them that way.

She had to admit to herself that knowing she might see the two handsome, bad asses' that had been frequently coming into the bar to eat dinner caused her heart to speed up and her nipples to harden when they walked in the door.

Race was a handsome six foot three or four inches tall, chocolate brown eyes, and the man had serious muscles clearly visible under his cut. He began wearing a new patch on the front of his cut a week ago that stated President, Mother Chapter.

His friend War now sported a Vice President patch, and he was perhaps an inch taller than Race, but clearly the men worked out or did some heavy type of lifting to keep the muscles so defined. War had blue eyes and she liked to imagine that those eyes followed her when he was in the bar.

It didn't matter to her which man spoke to her, she was getting used to changing her panties in the employee bathroom whenever they were around. It sucked because she had no intention of getting involved with any man for a while at least, and definitely not a biker at that. She'd found that her hormones had other ideas, but she told herself she could control them. Darnell would get back on his feet and want to resume his position at the bar, and it would be time for her to move on.

The winery was hidden behind the small woods that she remembered so well while she had stalked the place to find vulnerable spots. It was a huge, old winery that had been closed for ten years now, so the township was probably glad to have it occupied, even by a group known to frighten the daylights out of John Q Public. The taxes would be minimal because of the building being obsolete and would cost a small fortune to have demolished, so everyone won in the deal when the Breed bought the place for pennies on the dollar.

The group had been pretty quiet since the fire, and she wondered if things had changed so drastically, or if they were just waiting to see if further attacks would begin once they'd settled into a new spot. As far as she was concerned, her enemy was dead, and according to Maisie, the people who killed Tuck had been killed in the explosion. Wolfman had enjoyed a lingering pain filled death, and her only regret was that she hadn't stuck her knife in his guts to deliver him into hell. The funerals were held all at one time, and she didn't bother to attend. Knowing she would have been smiling and clapping her hands while his Brothers grieved, kept her at the bar that day. Over the weeks, she had heard all about the funeral, and the vows of revenge from men who paid lip service to loyalty to the scum of the earth.

She'd become a sick bitch one night, she took a drive and saw the markers forming crosses as well as several tributes in the small patch of ground that the ashes of the dead had been buried under several tons of fill dirt and grass seed. She'd stopped the truck and gotten out to walk around the spot. The brilliant idea popped into her head, and she grinned as she pulled her jeans down and pissed in the middle of the square plot. That had been the last time she'd gone near the place, and thinking about how satisfied she felt after pissing on Wolfman's grave still made her smile. As far as she was concerned, it was over, and in a few months she would leave this place and not look back. Her revenge was complete.

She was still smiling in remembrance of that night as she pulled the van into the parking lot of the new clubhouse. The Prospects that looked inside the rear of the van had obviously called ahead, because there were three young men waiting for her, and began unloading her cargo as soon as she cut the engine.

The lot was filled with bikes and muscle cars. A dozen pick-ups were lining the back row, and she ended up parking next to a deep sapphire blue dual cab that had a lift kit under the body that was so tall, someone her size would need a ladder to get into the cab. She couldn't imagine any man tall enough to open the door and step into it, even with the silver running boards that covered the rocker panels.

She walked through the lot and admired the bikes, wishing she could bring her old Scoot from Kansas to enjoy while she was here. She had the Norton, Indian and the Harley with the suicide shift in storage back home. They had belonged to Mr. McCormick, the old man who left her the bar, and now they belonged to her. Her Sportster was in storage with them. It wasn't fancy, and it wasn't the top of the line, but Tuck had given it to her to learn to ride on, and she wouldn't give it up.

The front doors were wide open and she walked into the building, immediately feeling the cooler temperature, and shivered. There were people everywhere, her height was hindering her progress, but eventually she found herself at the bar in what used to be the wine tasting room and climbed up on a stool to see the crowd of people at the gathering. Big men, hairy men, short men with chains hanging from their pockets to their belt loops, Club patches plastered on almost every cut, and rockers listing the Chapter they were from were represented and had filled the room.

She saw at least three different club patches, so the Breed had invited affiliates to join in the celebration. The wisdom of that decision was yet to be determined to her way of thinking. A loud squeal from the back corner of the room drew her attention, and when she finally saw what was going on, she wished she hadn't seen or heard a thing.

One of the passarounds' named Noodle was getting a spanking. It was not so much a play full slap on her ass, as a true ass whipping. Two bikers had her bent over a table with her knees on the chair and her bare ass exposed while they took turns smacking her ass cheeks with their hands. River had spoken to the woman a few times when she came into the bar, but didn't actually know her. She was a tough woman with an even worse vocabulary than some of the bikers that came into town. River turned back to the bar. Watching the woman getting off on being spanked wasn't her idea of a good time.

Goody was behind the bar with Yo-Yo and a Lucifer's Breed brother that she didn't know. His cut had the name 'Flats' embroidered on the chest. She liked most of the women she'd met that were part of the club, but seeing the woman they called Queeny stomp into the space where Yo-Yo and Goody manned the beer flippers made her watch the evil bitch closely. The woman was pretty, but she was also a wanna be Queen Bitch, and the others sneered at her when she pretended to be busy while they conversed. Anyone watching could see that she was filing away every bit of information that she heard, and from the narrowed eyes Flats was staring at the woman with, River wasn't the only one that noticed her blatant eavesdropping.

Yo-Yo finally saw her sitting there and waved. She yelled over the noisy voices that she'd be right there, and River nodded. She wasn't in a hurry, but she planned to be gone from the place once the sun began to set. By that time most of the bikers that drank would have a good buzz going, and that's when shit usually went downhill fast. She wanted to be long gone before that happened.

CHAPTER 4

Winning the coveted number one and two spots at the top of the Breed hadn't been easy. They had faced stiff opposition from some of the Chapters that had been staunch Wolfman allies. Those happened to be the Chapters where their main income stemmed from selling dope, and most were still resistant to changing anytime soon. They would be brought into line, but it would take time.

In the weeks after the fire, the two men had become true brothers' in arms. The start of the year before the fire, there had been fifty brothers on the roster at any given time. After the fire when the body count was made, they had twenty eight men left and six women that were supported by the club and the brothers. There had been eighteen of the brothers that hadn't been around the clubhouse when it went up. They had been working at jobs, out on club business, or at home with their families.

No one mentioned the basement that had been occupied by several wasted brothers' and a couple of equally wasted females to the authorities, so they hadn't bothered to dig deeper to find and identify the other bodies. Luckily the bunker under one of the trailers had been left unscathed, and much of the Club's disposable assets had remained safe from prying eyes and the heat of the fire.

The official cause of the fire was listed as a gas leak, and no one disputed the findings. The club would deal with the rivals that caused the debacle with no help from outside sources. There was little doubt in the remaining members' minds that it had to be a rival MC that blew the place up and killed so many of their comrades, so the brothers' stayed vigilant, waiting for someone to claim responsibility. Only War and Gummi knew the truth, and neither would talk, for obvious reasons.

When Gummi left the club to work in town, War encouraged her to go. "You need to find a place where you feel safe, and this isn't the spot for you to stay. I'll miss you, but you have a chance to leave now and still find a good life. If you ever need me, you know where to find me." He'd kissed her on the forehead then dropped her off in front of the bar with her sack of possessions that she'd salvaged from the blown over trailers.

Race was sitting at the table with him on the balcony of the main room of their new clubhouse. The men had put a call out to get help for construction of the interior of the building, and two dozen brothers' from the Chapter clubs had shown up to help. Most of them had brought at least one prospect with him, and since then over half of the brothers' had expressed interest in staying on. The prospect count had been almost one hundred percent that were requesting a berth with the Mother Chapter. All in all, things were falling into place, and he and War made a damned good team.

He moved too quickly, and immediately regretted it. Two weeks ago he was challenged by one of the Chapter Presidents, and the man hadn't been easy to beat, in fact, he was now their Sergeant at Arms. The fight had taken quite a while, with neither man willing to quit, and Race had finally gotten a lucky solid punch to the brother's jaw, knocking him out before collapsing with a couple of broken ribs and sheer exhaustion. Race had decided that if the brother was tough enough to almost whip his big ass, the man needed to be an ally instead of someone waiting for him to turn his back for the knife. In spite of War's skepticism, he'd put Bam Bam's name up for the position, and the man was voted in. His ribs were a lingering memory of the day, and the doctor said he should be healed in a few more weeks.

So far, he hadn't regretted the decision, but he knew that War was keeping an eye on Bam Bam, just in case his aspirations got the better of him. There had been the percentage cuts too, and that had been a big problem, but the clubs would pay up, or lose their Chapters. Examples would be necessary, but unlike Wolfman, he wasn't demanding more than the normal percentage from each club Chapter. It was no wonder that a few that were ignoring the majority of club's examples and pulling out of the drug business. He had the go ahead from the majority to demand the Chapters change and invest their time and assets into acquiring more legitimate ways to produce income. Those that stayed for the meeting tomorrow would learn the fate of a Chapter that defied the majority's' rules.

As he was watching the crowd of people below where they sat, he spied the curvy waitress from Double D's and considered catching up with her later. If that fucker War wasn't watching her at the same time he was, he would hot foot his ass down to the bar and chat her up. This habit his dick had of swelling whenever he saw her was getting old damn quick. Yesterday he'd come back to the clubhouse and drafted Yo-Yo into sucking him off because the damn thing refused to let him forget seeing her. It hadn't helped to know that War had done the same thing with Rose. He hated the fact that they both wanted her, and he wasn't sure that he would step aside if War got her to fuck him first. That would cause a shit storm that he didn't want, but something about her drew him, and he didn't have the answer to the problem.

The men had already almost come to blows when War insisted that they all get tested for STD's. His argument that Dew Drop had been a known carrier of the clap and she was a needle user, was valid. Most of the passarounds were afraid to fuck the men that had enjoyed the woman's sexual favors before, and had brought their concerns to War. Today there were several bowls of condoms littering the tables and guest barracks in case the housecats bestowed their favors on some of the guests, or anyone else. That had caused more problems, but the home based brothers seldom argued over the protection nowadays. It was a good thing the County Health Department handed the things out like candy or the club would go broke buying condoms. Race grinned at the thought of a surcharge for sexual necessities. *Yeah, that would go over well.*

Kink pulled up a crate to sit on and rested his elbows on the wooden surface of the table, before he began talking. "It looks like a good crowd down there tonight. It's a good thing River brought some eats with her, and you gotta' give the woman credit, she brought a keg and a case of Jack to welcome us to our new home. Classy bitch, that's for sure."

War and Race gave him dirty looks and he laughed. "So that's the way the wind blows, I'll be damned." He looked down to the bar and saw Mambo standing next to her, and whatever he said had made her laugh. He looked at War and then Race and shook his head. "You two have it bad, she's cute and all, but I like a woman that knows her place. Did you ever see her toss someone out of that bar? She kicked ol' Inca's knee and damn near slit his throat when all he did was pull her in close for a little smooch. Up till then, I planned to let her suck my cock after hours, but seeing her with that knife to his throat changed my mind. With my luck, she'd bite my dick off, and that would be a damn shame. Goody might cry and shit if that happened."

War turned his attention back to Kink, the man was walking a thin line with him to begin with, and his arrogance was grinding on his nerves. If the man kept making comments about River, well, the drop was close to fifteen feet from where they sat, the man might live to regret his dumb ass words.

To be fair, Kink was a handsome son-of-a-bitch, and the women liked him well enough, but War didn't like him, never had. Making an example of him wouldn't bother him a bit, but he wasn't going to start shit over a woman. Especially one that no one in the place had a claim on. He decided to be diplomatic, or at least his version of diplomacy.

"She took over the bar for Mambo's Uncle and Aunt, he tells me that she's honest and has been good for business. If she has the balls to put a brother in his place, I have no issue with her methods. As far as I know, she isn't fair game, and until she declares she is, or she gets claimed, don't fuck with her. She's not one of us and we don't need more trouble right now." He looked back to the crowd of people and shook his head when three girls walked in the door. "You need to get down there and check those twitchy assed kids that just came in. Those girls are jailbait from the tender looks of them, and we don't let them in here, remember?"

Kink followed his gaze and pointing finger then sighed. "Fuckin' high school sluts, might do them good to get fucked by real men instead of high school football players and pretty boys, but I'll get rid of them." He got up and went to the fireman's pole that one of the brother's had found in an abandoned firehouse and installed for shits and giggles in the clubhouse. He waved as he wrapped his legs around the thing and slid down out of sight.

War watched him make his way to the middle of the room where five men had surrounded the fresh meat. He looked at Race and said, "I think we might have a problem with Kink. If I see him fuckin' with underage girls, I'll bust his stupid head in. Three days ago he was so out of it, he couldn't stand on his own and pissed himself sitting out front. He's still doping and he can't keep his mouth shut for shit. Did you see his damn eyes? The bastard is high as fuck."

Race had been silent during Kink's short visit with them. The man never came around them when he was high because he knew he was close to getting busted about the shit he smoked and sometimes shot up on. "I agree. If he lasts the week-end, we'll toss him in the distillery and dry his ass out, if that don't work, he's gone. You know he was after information, and I think we probably gave him more than he expected, right?" War looked puzzled until Race jerked his head in the general direction of the bar. "We have the same taste in women, he picked up on that quick for a man that appears to be too fucked up to remember his own name. I think our friend has more to hide than his love affair with H, and I think we should keep an eye on his coming and going for a while just in case I'm right."

War nodded his head and said, "Got it covered. Joey's been his shadow for a week. So far nothing out of the ordinary, but some of the brothers have mentioned that Kink must have a sugar momma stashed somewhere. The man always has cash and as far as anybody knows, he doesn't have a job in the private sector."

Race sighed, that's all they needed, a fuckin' mole to go with the other hundred things to get straightened out with the club. He looked around the renovations that had been done so far, and felt a sense of pride. There were twelve private rooms for the brothers to stay in and two large rooms downstairs equipped with rows of bunks for visitors. In the back of the building behind the kitchen area were more rooms that were occupied by the women. They shared rooms with two women in each, and everything seemed to be working well so far. Ruby was the oldest female that lived in the clubhouse, and she had her own room. She was the widow of the President before Wolfman took the reins of the MC and no one fucked with the feisty, old broad. She stayed in her rooms most of the time nowadays, especially when they had visitors. Her former beauty had faded and she suffered from dementia at times, but she was respected by the brothers, and the housecats knew not to fuck with her, or their days with Lucifer's Breed were numbered.

Race decided to broach the subject that wouldn't leave his brain or his cock alone for more than a few hours at a time. "We need to get something out in the open. You and me are both attracted to her and I'm not one to fight over a piece of ass, but that particular piece of ass has my fucking dick's attention, and the bastard pays attention when she walks her ass in the room. River hasn't given me the go ahead or I'd have fucked her where I found her and had five minutes with no interruptions."

War looked down to where River sat at the bar, yeah, they had a problem. "That's the fuck of it. I get hard seeing her and my damn hands itch to strip her and drive as deep as I can get inside of her. The little bitch smiles and, fuck, look at her down there."

Mambo and Flats were talking to her and they had her laughing so hard that her head was thrown back. They could see her creamy throat and a slight amount of cleavage from the angle where they sat above the bar.

"I'm not gonna lie to you man, if she'd give me the time, I'd be making a meal out of her myself. If you've got a solution, I'm willing to hear it. I see her and all I can think of is spreading her out then eating that pussy until she screams for me to fuck her. So I don't know what to tell you. I want her." War had to readjust his cock. Just talking about eating that sweet pussy had his cock at full mast, and the pressure of his jeans over the flesh of his cock was as close to torture as he wanted to get.

CHAPTER 5

River noticed that the sun was setting and decided it would be a good time for her to make her exit. She could pick up the empty keg on Monday and told Flats that she would pick it up later. She waved to the girls behind the bar, they smiled and gave her absent minded waves. The place was filled with so many people that River left her perch and began making her way to the door, hoping that she was headed in the right direction. Too bad Mambo had been dragged off to shoot darts with some of his brothers. He would have been a good crowd blocker for her to follow to the door.

Within minutes, she'd almost run into couples engaging in varying forms of sexual acts, and she knew that her face had to be red. Seeing three men standing around with their cocks hanging out of their jeans while a woman was on her knees with one cock in her mouth and her hands wrapped around the other two was a shock. The woman that was sitting straddled on one man's lap wasn't as shocking as seeing a man come up behind her and spit in his hand, rub it on his dick, then he bent at the knees and shoved his hard cock into the woman's asshole. River vaguely remembered that the woman's name was Trey and from the way she shoved back on the cocks filling her holes, the name wasn't much of a mystery, especially when a third man was pushing his cock into her mouth. She stopped moving after the second time she almost tripped on the legs of women kneeling on the wooden floor sucking men's cocks.

She slowly turned in a circle hoping to see someone she knew that wasn't busy having their cocks sucked to ask for directions. On her second rotation, she saw the two men that made her draw in her breath. Race and War stood side by side waiting for her to notice them. She smiled and held her hands up and dropped them down.

"I'm vertically challenged. I don't know what you bikers eat when you aren't at the Double D, but even the shorter guys are giants when you're five foot four. I'm trying to find the door, but as you can see, I can't." She grinned at her own expense. "I don't suppose you could point me in the right direction?"

Race shook his head with a smile. He bent down and the next thing she knew, she was straddling his waist with her knees and they were heading in the direction of the door. She looked at War, who was pacing their progress along side of Race. He wasn't scowling exactly, but he didn't look happy either.

She didn't understand why he was looking so grumpy, but she apologized anyway. "I'm sorry to be such a bother, I thought I'd better leave before it got dark and the real partying started. I only planned to stay for a few minutes to begin with, but I like to talk too much I guess and Mambo is hilarious when he starts telling jokes. I lost track of time."

She wanted to lean into Race's embrace and lick his neck. It was obvious that he'd shaved earlier because of the tiny nick she saw just under his jawbone. War had been trimming his beard lately and she knew that she needed to get out of this place before she did something stupid.

She felt them climbing steps and looked down. "Uh, I was leaving and I don't remember climbing stairs when I came in here." Race didn't answer her, and War was behind them, so she couldn't see his face, and he was as silent as his friend.

At the top of the steps, Race kept his hold on the cheeks of her ass and walked down the long, wide catwalk until they stood outside of a set of old iron clad doors. War pulled the door open and Race walked into the room still holding onto her. She could feel his hard cock pushing against her crotch and knew that she was wet between her legs if not from her nearness to him, then from the friction of his cock plastered against her clit.

The door closed behind War and Race sat her down on a table top, before making no effort to hide that he was adjusting his hard cock in his jeans.

She watched him reaching down into the waistband of his jeans and saw his hand moving the thick bulge of his cock. His hand moved up and out of his jeans, and she looked up into his eyes that were half closed. His nostrils were flared and he was breathing a bit heavier than he had been before he picked her up.

"I'm heavier than I look, I hope your back isn't hurt from carrying me around like that."

The man actually rolled his eyes and War snickered. They reached for chairs and she would have sworn that they had practiced moving in sync if they hadn't looked at each other as they flipped the chairs around so they could straddle the seats to rest their arms across the backs and shrugged.

"Are you two sure that you aren't related or long lost twins or something? I've read about twins that mirror each other just like you two seem to do. It's kinda hard to miss."

War grinned and Race smiled, but there was no answer to her question, so she sat back on her hands and waited for them to say something. War finally began talking, and then she was the one to remain silent.

"We have a problem and you are the only one that can fix the problem, so here it is. Race and I seem to have this mirror personality, as you call it, and we find that we're both attracted to you." Race nodded but said nothing. "We want to know which one of us you are attracted to, and once you choose, the other of us will bow out."

She couldn't have heard him correctly. They brought her up here to give her a choice between the two of them? It had to be the singular craziest thing she'd ever heard. How would a woman with experience choose between handsome, sexy and well, handsome and sexy? To ask her to pick between them was nuts. She had zero experience with sex or men at more than an arm's length before, and she had no intention of choosing one of them over the other. There was no choice to make, she wouldn't be here much longer, and she didn't want to get involved with a biker anyway.

They were staring at her, waiting for her to say something, she shook her head. "I don't know what to say here. I can't do that. You're both very handsome men, I'm sure you know that you're attractive, but I'm not what you need." She didn't expect Race to growl at her answer.

He was brief in his question. "Why not?" War nodded at Race's inquiry.

She shook her head at them. "I won't be here much longer, I'll be leaving as soon as Darnell is back on his feet. Not to mention, I would never get between friends like the two of you seem to be. I think you both are equal in my eyes. How would I choose? How would any woman with blood running through her veins choose? The only big difference I see at all is blue eyes or brown. And, I don't know, but I, no, just no."

War clipped out his questions and she wasn't prepared for it. "Where do you have to go that's so important? Either one of us could keep you happy in bed. And you wouldn't have to work if you didn't want to, so tell us. Why are you leaving the area?"

She shook her head, not knowing what to tell them. The truth would get her dead, jail, or worse. She wasn't really worried about going to jail. Bikers took care of their own business, didn't they? She might wish for death before they were finished with her, and she wasn't about to take that chance. It was time to pull her head out of her ass, they weren't for her, neither one of them were. *Dammit.*

"Where I go and what I do when I get there, isn't your business or concern. I might be going back to a husband or kids, did that ever occur to you?" She didn't like the ugly look that came over War's face, nor the scowl that she saw on Race.

"Look, I have plans and they don't include a man, so as flattered and tempted as I am, I respectfully decline the offer." She hopped down from her perch on the table and started for the door.

She got maybe five feet away from the men when she was grabbed around the waist and hauled up against a hard, muscular body. War's breath wafted over her neck, and his words sent a shiver down her spine.

"Not so fast Shorty, you haven't given us a chance to make our case. What's the harm in letting us try to persuade you into changing your mind? You can give each of us a chance and pick who you want, if looks aren't a factor. Hell, just watching you walk away made my dick stand up and if it had hands, the fucker would have clapped in appreciation. Look over there at poor Race, he's been hard since we saw you walk in the doors earlier tonight. I wanted to rip Mambo's head off his shoulders and stuff it up his ass because he made you laugh. This feeling isn't going away, so what do you have to lose?"

His lips nibbled their way up her jaw line and she let a small moan escape. What would it hurt to enjoy having a man instead of fighting the attraction? She could always leave when she was ready. When his hands cupped her breasts and pinched at the nipples that were hidden under her bra and shirt, her head laid back on his chest as his lips continued to explore her neck. She opened her eyes and was startled to see Race staring at her. His brown eyes seemed to blaze as he watched War seducing her. She closed her eyes and took two deep breaths before pulling out of War's embrace.

"This isn't fair to either of you, and I, I have obligations elsewhere. You guys are potent but again, I need to leave before this goes further."

Race was shaking his head and she stopped backing away when he stood up, and said, "Stop. I've been nice and all here, War has been giving you a little taste of pleasure 'cause your nipples are hard enough to poke out like they are. What's wrong Shorty, are you afraid that you might like what one of us would do to you? I bet that pussy is creaming your panties, and if I stuck my hand down your pants right now, your clit would be standing at attention. Should I check? You know, just to prove to all of us that I'm right?"

He would have won the bet, but she couldn't get tangled up with them, neither one of them. No matter how tempting, no matter how she could feel her stomach clench whenever they were near. It was time to bring out the show stopping conversation. "So let me tell you what this is like from my point of view. You want me to choose between the two of you, and are willing for me to give you both a whirl in bed. The one that I pick will marry me and have a few kids, and act like a real grown up, is this what I'm hearing here?" She almost smiled at the twin, narrow eyed stares and tightened lips. "Or is this a case of lust until you lose interest, and the other man might take sloppy seconds, if he hasn't found another slut to take his interest? Either way I get to be passed from one man to another, possibly someone not in this room. Is that what you're offering?"

They didn't know that she was only half serious, and she wasn't going to let them know that if she had met them elsewhere, or circumstances had been different, she might have given in to the lust she felt for them. She shook her head. "Sorry guys, I'm not one of your passarounds, and I'm not interested in becoming one. Thanks, but no thanks. If I wanted to end up like some of the housecats I see here, I could have done that years ago. I'm not better than them, I just have different ideas about sex and how I value myself."

She didn't wait around to hear the bitching about her gauntlet. The part about marrying really pissed them off from the looks they gave her, and as much as she might regret leaving the two of them alone without trying them out, well, it was necessary. She almost ran to the door, pulled it open and was halfway down the hallway by the time she heard the door open again. She sped up going down the stairs and wished she had the time to admire the renovations the group had done to the old building. She paused at the last landing and looked out into the room, deciding to follow the wall to the door and make her escape. Her plan worked, even when she dodged couples, and men three deep watching an arm wrestling challenge going on. As long as she kept sight of the wall, she was headed in the right direction. When she reached the door, she looked up towards the balcony and saw the men that had been playing on her mind. They were watching her, and for some reason seeing them so far away made her sad to be leaving. It was for the best, but knowing that didn't lessen the regret she was feeling.

It was a long drive back to town, but she turned the upbeat music station on, and shouldn't have been surprised that she quickly turned the channel. She needed blues tonight. Happy, dance in your seat music wouldn't cut it in the mood she was in.

It was early evening and she made the decision to stop off at Darnell and Dena's house. Luckily they were sitting on the front porch when she pulled into the driveway. She would see for herself what kind of progress Darnell was making. The old couple waved at her once she got out of the van and they could see who was visiting.

She saw the former robust bar owner and her heart sank. He was half the size that he'd been just weeks ago when she last saw him. She had to say something, he was trying to smile from the left side of his face which was still unmarked from the stroke. The right side of his face drooped as if half of his face had melted. It was hard to look him in the eye, but he'd always been a good employer, and he deserved her respect.

"Hi there, I was coming home from the housewarming party the Breed are throwing and drove down your street. I hope I'm not interrupting you on this beautiful night. It's a good night to sit outside though."

Della smiled and stood up almost running to the doorway. "Let me get you a nice glass of sweet tea, dear. Darnell and I have been staring at the lightening bugs and not much else, so you aren't interrupting a thing."

Before River could say a word to decline the tea, Dena was through the screen door and out of their sight. She turned and smiled at Darnell and saw he was trying to tell her something, so she leaned in close enough to try to lip read what she couldn't understand verbally. "Come on man, slow down. I have the time to get it right, so you're gonna have to work with me here."

He rolled his eyes and she burst out laughing. "Oh come on, cut me some slack here. I've never had to deal with your particular problem, but if I can decipher what Freddy Joe Barnes says when he's falling down drunk on the sidewalk, I can figure out what you're saying. Just consider me a not too bright kid and be patient. Okay?"

Darnell made a noise that sounded like the cross between a duck and a growling cat. She realized that he was laughing at her, and she grinned at him. He nodded, and she returned the gesture.

He began slowly. "Thank you for pitching in, Dena is dealing with me and my shit. Thought I was a dead man for awhile." He did his best to look towards the door to see if his wife was eavesdropping, but couldn't move that far. He jerked his left hand towards the doorway, and asked, "Is she there?"

River shook her head. "No, I'll watch for her."

The old guy nodded again and almost fell over trying to get closer to her to tell her, "She don't know, I'll be dead soon, doctor told me." He sat back trying to catch his breath. "I wanna sell the bar, she'll need income, not rich, sell the bar, she can move to the south with kids."

He seemed to go to sleep after that. She was deciding how this would impact her managing the bar. How long would it take to sell the place, and her second thought was regret that she was leaving, even though she knew she had to go.

Suddenly, he shifted in the wheelchair and reached his hand towards her. Once she took it, he thanked her. His speech was even more slurred than it had been, and she squeezed his fingers. "I'll help in any way I can."

His gaze stayed on her face and as if a light dawned, he startled her by saying, "Tuck, good kid, sorry. Mambo, we called." This time he did fall asleep and she was itching to ask him for more information, but drool was trickling down his chin, as he slept.

Dena came out of the house with a tall glass of sweet tea and handed it to her. She sat down in the chair she'd vacated, and the concern on her face towards River, made her want to cry. These people knew who she was. How that was possible she had no idea, but they could give her answers, and seeing Dena put her finger to her lips, stopped her questions before she could voice them.   She mouthed, "Later" and nodded her head as a young man in a prospect cut came out from behind the house, Dena introduced him as Harpo.

"I don't know what we'd do without him."

Her words made the young man blush, but he gave her a quick nod and took charge of Darnell's wheelchair. "Time for bed buddy, say goodnight to the pretty ladies."

River got up and held the screen door for him to push the chair through, and got a hasty "Thanks" for her help, as he pushed the chair into the house and disappeared down the hallway that ran alongside the living room.

Dena looked wrung out, but River wasn't leaving without knowing what she knew about her brother and his death.

"I'm sorry, but I have to ask you what you know about Tuck. I know he was here when he died, at the club I mean, so what happened? Please tell me."

The older woman was staring at the porch rail before turning her eyes towards River. "I only know what Darnell told me and it wasn't much." She drew a couple of deep breaths and a sip of her glass of tea, before talking. "Here it is. Darnell came home from the bar one night in a tizzy. When I cornered him, he broke down and told me about Tuck. He said that the kid had been killed for seeing Wolfman doing something that he shouldn't have. He'd been stabbed and left to rot on the side of the road, down by Second Street. Darnell was told that by Mambo and they found your number tattooed on the inside of the boy's ankle. Darnell called you, he and Mambo met you that night." She brushed her hand over her face and shrugged her shoulders. "That's all I can tell you. I don't have details, and I'm sorry for your loss, he was always nice to me and Darnell."

River had to ask, "Did you hear what Darnell told me about selling the bar?"

Dena just nodded and laid her head back on the cushioned chair back. "Yes, I was the one to bring it up. I guess he finally figured out that he wasn't going back and running it for a long while. The old bastard is so stubborn that I didn't dare start making plans to move us. Sure as hell he'd decide to stay put just out of cussedness."

River finished her tea and turned to Dena. "Thank you for the tea and being such a great employer, but thank you most for letting Darnell bring my brother home to me, he's all the family I had."

Saying goodbye, she walked off the porch and got back into the van. She drove on auto pilot to the bar. At least she had a reason and knew who had befriended Tuck's body and her that night. The place was dark, but something didn't seem right. There were two bikes behind the building, and they weren't one's she recognized. That wasn't unusual in itself, but why would they be parked in the back? The only thing she could think was that Maisie was in there, she'd been sleeping in the store room while she saved up money to get herself a place to live.

"Fuck, dammit, why does this have to get complicated now?" She didn't have her gun with her, all she had were her boot knives. She thought about calling the cops, but if Maisie was entertaining voluntarily and she called the heat down on them, it could create problems that she didn't need. "Shit, I know I'll be sorry for this, but she might need help."

She cut the engine and left the van in the narrow driveway between the road and the dumpsters. That way, there was no way for the bikers to leave on their rides. She had to climb out of the back of the van due to the fence being on one side and the building on the other with very little space on either side. Climbing over the top of the van was an experience she didn't want to repeat. If her mission wasn't so important, she would walk in the front doors and find out what was going on, but the building was dark. Maisie had her odd ways at times, but the woman was responsible. The alarm would be on and the little bell that rang whenever the door was opened would announce that she was there.

CHAPTER 7

The back door latch was broken, so she knew that whoever was inside, hadn't been invited in. She pulled the door open and almost knifed Maisie as the little woman was sliding out of the doorway. She almost knocked River over and opened her mouth when she saw the wicked knife, but she put her hand on River's chest and gave her a push back outside. The women hopped the concrete barriers that Darnell had put in after they'd found the last poisoned biker by his dumpsters. They ran a full block before they stopped for breath and River reached for the cell phone in her back pocket.

Maisie put her hand on the phone and shook her head. "No, not the cops, they're Breed, call War, he'll come and get them. They aren't from around here, but we need to let the club take care of them."

River was pissed but handed the phone over to her friend. "I don't have any of their numbers, if you do, go for it. They're going to pay for the damages those bastards are doing, I heard glass breaking." She sat with her back to the old storage garage that they'd taken refuge behind and tried to calm her breathing down. She noticed that she still held her boot knife in her fist and slid it back into the leather sheath inside the neck of her right boot.

Maisie made her call. "It's me, uh, Gummi. You know I've been working at the Double D, right? Well, here, River can tell you." She shoved the phone towards the woman that was giving her a dirty look. "Sorry, he sounds mad."

She took the phone and scowled at her little companion. She didn't wait for whoever was on the other end of the line to speak. "This is River over at the Double D, you have some brothers over here that broke into the place and are trashing it as we speak. You have twenty to get their asses out of there and bring your checkbook, you're gonna need it." She hit the end button and shook her head at Maisie.

"Don't ever let me hear you call yourself that damn name again. You don't have to kiss their asses' or suck their dicks anymore. Fuck them. You told me you wanted out and that you had permission to go. You are a beautiful, strong woman and don't you forget it." She took the woman by the shoulders and shook her a little.   "Maisie, I'll be leaving in a few weeks, I'd planned to ask you if you wanted to come with me. You can start over if you want and have a good life. I have a business and you'll have a job if you decide to come with me. You told me that you wanted to feel free. You can do or be whatever you want. It's up to you. I'm not your momma, or your actual boss. All I can promise you is that you don't have to grovel to anyone again if you seriously want to change your life."

The women grew silent and listened to the roar of bikes coming their way. Maisie grinned at River. "I've never heard anyone speak to Race like that before, even Wolfman showed him and War respect to their faces. He's gonna be madder than hell about the brothers trashing the bar, but he'll give you an earful about respect once he thinks on it."

River didn't bother to refute her claim. "If the demanding bastard has a problem with a woman asserting herself, well then I guess all I can say is, *fuck him.*" She remembered something. "I thought you said you were calling War, why did you call Race?"

Maisie shrugged. "I hit the wrong numbers and when I heard his voice, I got scared, he scares me. He must have used the old club's number for his cell phone, because that's the number I called."

The women walked back to the bar on the same path they ran away from it on. There were bikes were parked in front and two skinny prospects standing at the alley entrance watching the bikes. River walked up to the front door of the building and was blocked from entering by the young men.

"We're sorry, no one goes inside until I get the go-ahead." The kid with the scruffy beard was trying to be tough but polite, and the other one stood with his body in front of the door like he would stop anyone from entering with his life if need be.

"That's good, but I happen to be the manager of this place. I need to see the damage and my employee here will need to help me start cleaning it up. So you need to get permission or whatever, so we can start."

The kid was shaking his head and the other one mirrored his gesture. "Look lady, I'm sorry, but club business is going on in there, you stay outside until I get told different."

The women ended up sitting in the cargo hold of the van with the doors open, waiting to be granted permission to enter the building. The longer they waited, the madder River became. Maisie laid her head down on the thick moving pads that they used to keep food hot and bottles and other glassware from clinking together and breaking when they transported catered meals or made a liquor run.

The two young men watched her like a hawk or River would have gone over the fence and into the back door. She laid back on the pads next to Maisie, to rest her back and within minutes was asleep.

*****

Race watched War breaking his knuckles on Younger and Les. They'd left Mambo and Bam Bam back at the Club because of all of the out of towners running around there. The two men currently getting the hell beaten out of them had arrived to the area late and said they were thirsty. "No one would tell us where the clubhouse is, so we figured to get a drink, and then we'd find someone and persuade them to talk."

The sloppy drunk fuckers would feel their fuck up in the morning. In the mean time, they were all sitting with their thumbs in their asses waiting for the two men's president to show up. Once Race had found out where the two were from, he called Bam Bam, and told him to put the president of the Dixie chapter into a cage and get his ass to town. He was pissed and War had just knocked the second fucker out without working the mad out of his system. He heard the door open and saw Bam Bam wait for Glimmer to walk inside the bar before following him.

Glimmer obviously didn't see the problem. He walked over to the men on the floor and bent down to roll them onto their backs so he could get a good look at his brothers.

"What the fuck man, did you have to beat the hell out of them? Or did they go at each other again?"

Race took a drink of his beer and shook his head. "Come on over and have a seat, we need to talk."

Once Glimmer was seated, he looked annoyed, but he kept quiet.

Race took a deep breath and spoke quietly, but he got his point across. "We invited our brothers to celebrate the new clubhouse and for a summit. It was supposed to be a good time amongst brothers with common goals." He stood up, leaning his knuckles on the table between him and Glimmer. "You do not come to our place, our town, and turn your boys loose. We don't piss in our backyard and I'll be damned before I let any fuckers come here and take a shit in it. This bar is owned by a brother's elderly relatives. They've been good people and always welcomed the Breed. Tell me, how welcome will we be the next time we come to town? Not to mention when the brother finds out what happened, he's going to be looking for someone's blood."

Race stood up straight and began walking to the door, saying over his shoulder to Billy and Elton, "Get the prospects to clean it up in here and Bam, take Glimmer and his boys back to the distillery, they need to sleep it off, we'll settle this tomorrow."

War followed him out. His knuckles were bleeding from connecting with Les's teeth, but he wiped the droplets on his jeans and kept walking. Those ignorant fucks didn't give him the fight he was looking for and if he considered the mood he'd been in to start with, they got off lightly.

Race was mounting up and he was ready to follow suit, when he saw the prospects holding up the brick wall by the alley. One was facing towards the back of the building and his companion was grinning from the side profile War could see. He stomped over to the men and they straightened up to face him.

"Okay, what the fuck is more important to you? Watching the bikes or getting the hell beat out of you for not watching them?"

The young men flushed and when Trainer stood up straighter, War thought for a minute that he might get to work some more of the mad out of his system. If the boy wanted an ass whipping, he'd be challenging the right man for it. Instead the kid jerked his thumb back towards the alley, so War side stepped them and looked for himself.

Seeing the two women lying back on blankets pillowing their upper bodies, and recognizing those bodies gave him the reason for their distraction. River's shirt had slipped the top half of the buttons, and her ample tits were daring a man to bury his face between them. The lace cups only added enticement to the urge and he balled up his fists to keep from reaching out to her and helping himself. Maisie was curled up on her side facing the wall of the vehicle, but her ass was hanging halfway out of the cheek baring shorts that she was wearing.

The sound of Race's Scoot starting up made River twitch, when he twisted the throttle, she sat straight up wondering what was happening. It took mere seconds for her to focus on a pair of jean clad legs and an impressive bulge behind the tight denim, and for her to realize that she must have fallen asleep. She reluctantly looked further up at the man standing over the back of the van, and saw War staring back at her with that same look he wore earlier today at the clubhouse.

She realized that he wasn't looking at her face when she sat up. She looked down to where she thought his eyes were staring and gasped. Shit, her damn shirt had come undone and he was getting an eyeful of her breasts. She grabbed the sides of the shirt and began buttoning it up, making a mess of the row, only to start over when she realized she still had two buttons without holes to put them in. She had to break the silence, that stare and the way he licked his lips, tempted her beyond where she wanted to go right now. Especially given the place and the company watching to see what would happen.

War beat her to the punch. "The next time I find you like this I'm gonna take what's offered. I won't give a shit where, or who's watching." He stepped back and added, "Go home and take her with you, the boys will do clean up and lock it up for you tonight."

She hopped down from the van and started to demand to be allowed inside the bar now, but his next words stopped her.

"Do not fuck with me. I told you to go home. Do I need to take you there myself? I can guarantee that I'll keep you there for the night and probably most of tomorrow. So make up your mind, what do you want to do?"

River didn't know what made her do it, but she stomped her foot like a five year old and raised her voice at him. "You're not the boss of me, I'm a grown woman and you are just being a bully!" She pointed towards where the prospects were still standing, watching the entertainment. "You are the boss of them, you want someone to tell what to do, tell them." She clenched her fists and could barely contain her case of frustration towards him. She allowed the fingers in her hands to relax while she held out her arms and made shooing gestures with her fingers. "Go away, the next time something like this happens I'll call the police to deal with them."

The little witch kept doing that shooing thing with her hands and he'd about had enough. At the threat of calling the heat, well, there was only so much a man should be expected to take from a woman less than half his size. He moved in and lifted her up into his arms, sat down in the rear of the vehicle, and flipped her over onto his knees face down, bottom up. She screeched, but he ignored the noise and enjoyed the feeling of her wiggling body trying to escape his hold.

His hand rubbed over the thin material of her pants, cupping each cheek of her ass in turn before delivering a quick smack to each. She was making too much noise for him to talk to her so she would listen, so he gave her another ten good whacks on the ass. He felt her reach for his pant leg and pull it up, he knew she was going after his blade. "You think I'm gonna let you stab me with my own knife?"

He almost rolled her off of his legs when he reached over and grabbed her arm, bending it backwards. "Let it go or the arm will break. I don't normally have to tie a woman up, but if you keep doing this shit, I will. I don't know why some man hasn't taken you in hand a long time ago, but I don't put up with anyone talking to me that way."

Her arm relaxed enough for him to bring it up and hold it in the center of her back, before he really began wailing on her ass and upper thighs. Her screams had stopped altogether, and she was sobbing like her heart was breaking before he let her sit up.

He wiped the tears from her cheeks with his thumb. "Go home, River. Don't make me take you there, or you'll really hate me in the morning."

She nodded her head, knowing that she couldn't trust herself from saying some things that would earn her more than a severe spanking. Her ass was on fire, but at least she was still alive to know it. She had to grab the door to get her balance, before standing aside while he walked away from the van. Maisie had been huddled in a tight ball as close to the backseat as she could get all the time War was busting her ass, and if she hadn't seen the tears running down her face, she might have been embarrassed for the woman to have witnessed her humiliation.

"Hey, it's all right. Let's go to my place, we'll grab something to eat on the way." The answering nod was her only reply, so River climbed back in, and shut the cargo doors, before climbing over the bench seat, so she could take the driver's seat.

CHAPTER 8

Race had circled around and came back when he realized that War wasn't with him. He stopped his bike in front of the gawking prospects. They weren't happy when they got the jerked thumb gesture and had to go inside, but he wasn't very happy when he saw River getting her ass spanked either. Not that he objected to the smart mouthed object of his desire being turned over a knee. His objection was that it wasn't his knee.

When she disappeared into the back of the van he continued on his way. War was rubbing the hand that he'd used on her ass and Race grinned to himself. River just might decide that he was the better choice after this little run in. After all, Race wasn't the one that had spanked her now was he?

Not that he wouldn't slap that ass if she got too lippy, he would do it, and he'd enjoy it too. Hopefully she'd learned from dealing with War, and acted a little friendlier the next time he saw her. His mood was much lighter than it had been a half hour ago and he twisted the throttle, time for a beer or two, and he'd deal with the serious shit tomorrow.

War caught up with Race a mile from the clubhouse. His mood was as black as he could remember, and he wasn't sure how he was going to cope with tonight's events. River was driving him nuts. His cock was barely allowing him think, until the blood finally left the fucker and traveled back to his head where it belonged.

War pulled into the road and kept going. He had to cool his shit before he got back to the meeting. There were two clubs that would have to be shown that National Club rules superseded their petty shit. Of course they had to be cronies of Wolfman, but he was dead, from his own arrogance and stupidity. Race would need back-up to put the seriousness of their agenda firmly into the brains of the fuckers. He smiled, anticipating the coming fight.

A bat flew across his chest, hitting his arm and bouncing off. *Fuck, pay attention, dumbass.* The little critter was small, but where he hit would leave a bruise by tomorrow. Damn, that stung. *Fuck it*, he opened it up on the straight road in front of him and let the wind take his mood away for a while.

Race heard War's scoot go past the turn off and shook his head. He almost felt sorry for the poor bastard.

Mambo wasted no time coming over to where Race sat to ask what happened. Once he explained the evening's happenings, Mambo had his fists clenched and the man wanted retribution for his family. "Why wasn't I included in the meet and greet with those fucks? You knew that my family owns the place, since when did we coddle a motherfucker? I want a piece of them."

Race nodded his head in agreement. "The first reason is that when River called, she gave us very little time to get there before she threatened to call the boys in blue. You were nowhere to be seen at the time." He nodded towards the younger man with the pissed off look on his face and gave him what he wanted. "We'll be bringing this up at the summit tomorrow, and if they don't pay up for damages with a little extra for everyone's time and trouble, there's a couple of nice bikes still parked behind the Double D. Or you can beat their asses, depending on how they act, maybe both. Although there's not much left to beat after War got done with them tonight."

Race eyed Mambo for a minute and decided to give the man a heads up on tomorrow's agenda. "You know that the chapter they come from is still dealing dope as their main income. Their Prez is currently sleeping it off in the distillery, along with his boys. Tomorrow they will be the poster boys for the rest of the club." He shrugged. "They are the examples that we needed to demonstrate that you don't want to fuck with us. You'll get your retribution, one way or the other, you have my word."

Mambo stared at him for a few seconds and nodded. "As long as I get a shot at them, I got no problems. What kind of bikes are we talking here?"

Over the next hour they drank draft beers and discussed the possible uses for two extra Scoots, and what kind of cash the bikes might be worth. That led to talking about upgrades and Springer front ends versus stock, and their conversation drew several other brother's attentions and comments.

Race stood up and headed for his room above the bar. He was tired as hell and still horny. Seeing Goody standing behind the bar was a stroke of luck. He was surprised that she wasn't occupied with someone else tonight. When he cut over to see if she might be interested in spending a few hours in his bed, he didn't see War making his way toward the bar too. They met standing right in front of her.

As they stared at each other, Goody laughed. "Can I interest you boys in something good?" She licked her lips eyeing the two of them. "I think I can make it worth your while, if you have the time."

Race made his decision. Fuck it, if War didn't want a piece of her tonight that was on him. The other women were busy tonight and he needed to bury his cock into something warm and feminine. He nodded and Goody reached out her arms for him to help her over the bar. He didn't bother putting her down on her own feet. He handed her over to War, who dropped her over his shoulder and started walking towards the stairs. She grabbed onto Race's cut as War carried her past him.

"Come on, I'll give you a peek into Goody's box."

Race grinned and followed them up the steps. Watching the way, she patted War on the ass and reached her hand down the back of his pants to squeeze the man's ass cheeks was entertaining. War stumbled, especially when she straightened up, out away from his back while reaching for Race.

He reached around and turned the door handle to let them all enter the room.

Goody was as good as her reputation. War dropped her on the bed and she started working on his pants to get them open. Once she'd gotten her hands onto his thick cock, she lost no time in giving it a kiss and that led to stretching her mouth over the head and down as far as she could go.

Race dropped his cut on the hook behind the door and began striping his clothes off. She might be happy sucking War's cock, but he wanted her pussy clamping over his. He reached for the box of condoms on the nightstand and tossed one to War, just in case the need arose. This wasn't the first time they'd shared a woman and Goody was the kind of woman that liked her sex hot and filling.

War pulled his hips away from her reach and watched her lips pout as he took one of her favorite toys out of her grasping fingers and mouth. "Strip," was all he had to say to get her motivated into pulling the cut off tank shirt she was wearing over her head. She shimmied out of the thin material covering half of the cheeks of her ass, leaving her heeled shoes on her feet.

Race laid back on the bed and pulled her hair to redirect her head towards his cock, and she made a humming sound as she opened her mouth to receive his dick. "That's right, just for a minute, 'cause I'm gonna tear that pussy up tonight, no fuckin' mercy."

War wasted no time in rummaging in the crap that Race had scattered in the bedside drawer looking for lube. He found a small pillow pack of lube after moving a small handgun and a checkbook. Thinking that Race was an unorganized slob crossed his mind, but hearing Goody whine when Race pulled her head off of his cock got his attention back where it belonged.

Her ass was at the edge of the mattress and his lubed fingers began sliding into the slit towards her back hole. He saw Race putting a condom on his dick and scissored his fingers while two were deep in her heated tunnel.

"Damn Goody, you feel tight as fuck tonight, slow down a little or I won't get you wide enough and you know how that feels when it happens. Mine isn't one of them pencil dicks you're used to dealing with, remember?"

She twitched trying to stop her hips from demanding more from his fingers, but he refused to give her more until she settled down. He lifted her over Race's hips and put his fingers back into use widening her asshole. She immediately sat back on her heels and lowered her cunt onto Race's cock. War added a third finger and she grabbed fistfuls of Race's chest hair while she worked her hips up and down trying to seat herself completely onto his length.

He pulled his fingers from her hole and wiped them on the sheet as he tore the wrapper open with his teeth. He waited for her to get a good few strokes on Race before he caught her on the upstroke and let her slide down with his cock, finding the warmth of her asshole. It took a bit to get his dick inside of her body and he rested for a minute before pulling back so Race could slam his cock deep.

War grabbed her tits and gave the nipples a few hard squeezes, before he let them go and pulled her hips down when he felt her body start to clench deep inside.

Race reached down and began rubbing her clit with his fingers, and she screamed, grabbing her tits and squeezing them as she came. It took one more up and down stroke for the men before they followed her with her body still twitching and jerking as they filled her completely, each coming and shouting as they spurted cum into the latex tips of the condoms.

War got up and pulled the condom from his softening dick. He tossed it into the trash bag by the wall, and grabbed his clothes on the way to the door. The pressure was off his balls, but his mind was elsewhere and he didn't like it one bit. He walked naked into the hallway and to his own room with no one around, not that he gave a shit. Anybody within hearing distance would know what had gone on in Race's room. Hell, it went on in the main room downstairs everyday with some people. *So why do you feel like you did something that you need to hide?* He'd come in from his ride and decided what he needed was to get a piece of ass and relieve some of the pressure from his sexual need. Race just happened to have the same need, and fuck, he was confused. All the time he was buried in Goody's tight ass, he was wishing she was a smart mouthed, little woman with the bluest eyes he'd ever seen instead. *Face it dumb ass, the little witch has your mind on her, but you proved tonight that she wasn't leading you around by your dick, right?* It took a while, but he finally fell asleep.

Goody offered to stay the rest of the night and give him a "good morning to brighten his day," but he declined with a swat on her ass.

"I know that you're ready for round two, but I'm so fuckin' tired I won't be worth it for you to waste your time. Go find a couple of brothers that have the energy to enjoy your assets and thank you for sharing." He grinned from the bed that he hadn't left as she put her clothes on and let herself out of the door.

Well that was what you needed, right? He rolled over and sat up while he removed the latex from his dormant dick. *You horny fuck. Son-of-a-bitch.* Fucking Goody had taken the edge off, but not enough to make his brain feel good about it. Once she was seated on top of his cock, he'd closed his eyes and imagined that it was River bouncing her ass over him, while War filled her asshole. Taking her tits in his hands had been a mistake. Where Goody's tits were pert and proud, River's tits would be an overabundant handful. He imagined her nipples beading up and ready to be sucked and *fuck. Oh hell no*, he didn't need another hard on, he needed to sleep.

He ended up rising and taking a shower, where he jacked off, finishing his fantasy of River begging for their cocks to fill her. By the time he stumbled back to his bed, he could finally sleep and it took no time for his body to shut down. Picturing his arms filled with River sleeping beside him, gave him comfort as he cradled his pillow and slept.

CHAPTER 9

River backed the van from the alley and drove it to her place. She now had a small trailer in an RV park that she rented by the week, and after a dinner of thick beef burgers and fries, she and Maisie shared the double bed for the night.

River woke up just as dawn began and she watched the darkness being replaced by light grey and pink storm clouds from the window next to the tiny table that seated two people. She was on her second cup of coffee and was signing the letter that she'd just finished, when Maisie walked into the area from the tiny hallway. She smiled and offered a cup of coffee to the sleepy eyed woman, before re-reading the letter, and putting it into the addressed envelope next to her on the table.

Maisie was in a talkative mood and wanted to re-hash over what had happened last night. There was no shutting her up, so River let her talk while she got ready for the day.

"Those men last night, I should have told War what they were saying, but when he beat on you, I figured that they deserved what happens to them today at the meeting. He really shocked me sister, I never saw him hit a woman before. He was always kind to me."

River frowned at her own reflection in the mirror while she listened and pulled her hair into a high ponytail. The silence must be Maisie waiting for her to say something, but she really didn't know what to say, so she gave the generic, "Oh?" for her contribution to the conversation.

It seemed to satisfy Maisie, since she continued the subject. "Oh yes, I mean, I don't want anything bad to happen to the club. Now that Wolfy and his dogs are gone I mean, but if being one of the leaders has gone to his head enough to make him beat on a woman, especially one that isn't in the club, I guess they get what's coming to them."

River hung her head over the sink, she was having a hard enough time admitting to herself that the spanking hadn't hurt nearly as much as it had been intended to. In fact, when she'd tried to gain her freedom and put one of her legs down to find the pavement for a foothold to escape and that big hand had landed on the space between her legs…she shook her head. No way would she admit that she found pleasure in having her ass spanked like that. Not even to Maisie.

"It didn't hurt nearly as bad as I made it out to be. I thought you could tell that I was screaming so he'd think he was being effective. I must be a better actress than I thought." She grinned at the other woman and leaned over to whisper, "He hits like a girl." She sobered and made the decision to repeat her offer to Maisie of a new life, away from here.

"Last night I told you that I have a business and a place to live. I meant what I said, you'll be more than welcome to leave with me when I go. With your help, my reason for being here is over with and I won't leave you unless you tell me that's what you want me to do." She patted her shoulder and walked out into the crisp morning air.

*****

Maisie didn't give her an answer that day and River didn't press her. If she decided to go then great, if she wanted to stay, then it would be her choice. The bar was slow for a Sunday evening, but with the Breed having their meeting, it wasn't a big shock. Locals and a few visitors came in, but all in all the night was uneventful. Even the usual drunks didn't give her grief when she pushed the last ones out of the front door and locked it behind them.

Maisie was cleaning the kitchen, so River decided to go ahead and get the nasty chore of cleaning the bathrooms over with. The last time she'd been the unlucky one to clean the bathrooms, she'd found used condoms on the floor and broken drink glasses too. The drain in the middle of the floor was a godsend. If the place was a real sty, all she had to do was spray the place down with antibacterial stuff and hook up the short hose to the hot water spigot under the sink to blast it off.

The back door slammed shut as she turned the corner with her hands full of rubber gloves and the water hose. She caught a glimpse of half of a man's shoulder exiting the building and she dropped the items in her hand to check and make sure the door locked behind the late patron. She opened the bathroom door and dropped the wedge shaped block of wood to hold the door open before noticing the smell. She pulled on the long sleeved, rubber gloves and walked over to grab the trash, stopping in her tracks when she saw a man sitting on one of the toilets. She didn't recognize him, but that wasn't what alarmed her as much as the fact that he was obviously dead. He had to be a biker, the cut was unmistakable, even if his overgrown beard and the many large skull rings didn't decorate his fingers. "*Fuck.*"

"Maisie." She had to clear her throat to raise her voice. "Maisie."

She heard her before she saw her come into the hallway. "I'm not cleaning the toilets again, it's your turn, remember?" She stopped smiling when River pointed her finger towards their unwanted visitor.

"Oh shit, that's Glimmer, I've seen him with Wolfman before." She shook her head and backed away. "Not good at all. How did he get in here? He can't be in here." She grabbed her arm and pulled her into the hallway. "River, we need to get rid of him. His club will burn the place to the ground. Everyone with him is the same, they are like rabid dogs. You think Wolfy was bad? These guys brought him the slaves to work the strip club and the shed that you burned down. They used to talk about it upstairs at the old clubhouse."

River nodded in understanding. It stood to figure that the longer she stayed in this place, the more shit hit the fan. It had all been going too well and it appeared that she was right to question their good fortune. "Let's finish our normal chores and think about how to do this. All I saw was a man's shoulder, his tat was kind of a generic percent sign on the back of his arm, but I couldn't identify him."

She cleaned the women's bathroom and left the cleaning equipment in the men's bathroom out of the way so they'd have room to manipulate the two hundred pound biker's body when they were ready.

Her plan was fairly simple; the hard part would be moving his dead weight. They took two of the busing trolley's and taped them together with silver Duct tape and locked the wheels so the thing wouldn't move from where they left it next to the body. It took several attempts to get his upper torso up and over the top of the carts, and both women were winded by the time they got him onto the table so he could be moved. The cause of Glimmer's death was the large hole in the back of his skull where it had been beaten in with something heavy.

As they rested and then cleaned the room around the trolley, River couldn't help but say. "We can be thankful that he wasn't killed in here, can you imagine the mess that would have made?"

Maisie nodded in agreement. "You know what? I think I'm tired of hauling dead men around. I'm going to take you up on your offer. I thought I'd stick around to see if Mambo might want to settle down." She shook her head. "But there's a lot of history for both of us to get past and the more time I have to think about it, I'll be ready to leave when you are."

The weather was both a blessing and a curse since it had began to rain and sleet as they rolled Glimmer out of the back door and shoved his body into the bed of River's pick-up. The canvas top and tailgate were back in place while the women made sure the bar was clean and everything was in order for the next day.

River told Maisie, "This is your last night here, so grab your stuff and let's go. You're not the only one tired of this place. We leave in two days. I'd leave tomorrow, but if someone starts nosing around, we're just a couple of innocent women with nothing to hide. Right?"

Maisie laughed. "Oh yeah, we're just a couple of little women, what could we possibly do to an overweight, six foot tall bad ass? We are just as puzzled as whoever might ask."

They were headed out of town when a police cruiser sailed past them with his lights strobing in the icy sleet. River watched her rearview mirror until the lights were no longer visible and breathed deeply. They drove past the old winery and weren't surprised to see that no one seemed to be around the gate that was closed. The cage sitting just inside the gate held a couple of prospects, but in the dark of the night with the sleet coming down sideways such as it was, the women weren't real worried that they might be seen or recognized.

A mile from the Winery, River backed her truck up in the grassy spot overlooking the river that was still flowing swiftly. Winter was just beginning here and it would take a lot more cold weather than this to slow the current of the water. There was no traffic and no houses on this particular stretch of road, so it made an ideal dumping ground for Glimmer's body.

They watched as his weight carried him rolling over and over to the bottom of the steep hill and into the muddy riverbank. He was in God's hands now and they could breathe a sigh of relief.

Back at the trailer, they had celebration shots of whiskey and while River took a shower, Maisie must have been more tired than she acted, because the woman was snoring on the loveseat when she came out of the tiny cubicle. She tossed a blanket over her and left the small light on over the stove.

The air was cool, but River felt frozen to her bones. The hot shower had helped, and the shot of Jack had given her belly warmth, but it didn't change how she felt. When had she become so hard? Now that it was over, how could she find a dead guy, move him to a location where no one would think to look for him for days and still smile? Did the life of a human being mean so little to her since she'd come to this place for revenge?

Face it girl, it's time to go home, make some life choices and stick to them. The only glitch that she could see was if the people running the bar back home didn't want to leave. *Then what are you going to do, genius?* She rolled over and closed her mind off with a quick, *'shut it'.* She conjured up images of Race and War, and their lips, but it took a long time for her to fall asleep.

CHAPTER 10

There were over a hundred bikers at the winery for the summit and as the host Chapter, their people were outnumbered by a third, but no one seemed to want a direct challenge, so the initial hour and a half was easy going. It was when it came time to lay out the new agenda the problems began, but Race had anticipated their response. War stood behind him and four of the Chapter leaders opted to approve the agenda, but there were two factions that were resistant to any change in Lucifer's Breed MC policy.

One was Glimmers club and Race began with that. "I know there's resistance to change, but you have to decide, what's gonna happen when your kid gets some bad shit from someone? You're gonna take care of that business man, right? Times are changing, soon weed will be legal everywhere, a smart group would be getting ready to set up for that. Premium shit rakes in major bread and if you have brothers as businessmen in a legit business, hell who knows what the take would be. They're using 'J' for all kinds of shit, from clothes to medicines for sick kids. Think about it.

"From now on, you'd better be a diabetic if you want to bring a needle in here. If I have to personally make an example of someone who thinks I'm fucking with them, I'm not against making my point out of him.

"I realize things have been lax around the group, but that's changing. You come into our town and start shit like what happened last night, you're gonna lose more than your Scoot like those two did. I don't disrespect your turf, you don't get a free pass in ours. Now the floor is open for business."

Petty squabbles turned into chest thumping and men broke out in fistfights. Race let the small shit pass, there were too many brothers in the room to start too much large scale shit. There would be fines for those that threw punches during the meeting. He couldn't allow the disrespect to go unpunished. So went the day, arguments and agreements, discussions about businesses and financing. All in all it was a good day.

By Sunday night, most seemed to be in agreement to at least explore the possibility of changing income by members becoming businessmen in various forms. Race was feeling smug, until War and Elton told him that Glimmer was nowhere in the compound and his lieutenants had no idea where he disappeared.

"I don't like this, his boys over there? Why aren't they looking under the bushes for the Prez?" War had been watching the table full of members of the Dixie Chapter, and they all seemed a little too calm about the disappearance of the leader of their club. "I had Pete check on their bikes and Glimmer's Scoot is still in the parking lot."

Race had noticed that the Dixie boys seemed to be having a good time without supervision tonight, not to mention he hadn't seen Glimmer in since yesterday. He nodded to the table on his right.

"Prowler is here with his brothers and he's been shitfaced since he got here. That whore he brought with him is a bumper and she must have gotten her fix an hour or so ago, because she's downright friendly with Ol' Glimmer's vice. You see the way Prowler's smiling her way and she keeps looking back at him?"

Bam and Billy came over to join them and War stood propping up the wall while the men discussed the weather conditions. They concluded that most of the Breed would be staying on another day or two to let the roads clear enough for the bikers to leave for their home turf.

Bam waited for Billy to leave with Elton and told Race and War, "Pete thought he saw two people riding with Dixie rockers tonight before it started to rain. He was coming back from a beer run in Cass City, but didn't think anything of it. He said it had just gotten dark, but one of the bikes might have had two people on it. He wasn't paying attention."

He nodded at Race's question. "Ideas on who?"

"An hour or so before the meeting, Merc and Pauly came in with wet hair and they left water where they stood at the bar when they got a beer. I'd say those two are the ones I'd put my money on."

War piped up from the side. "Nice, so are we thinking the roaches are eating each other in a power grab?" He watched the woman plop her bony ass onto Merc's lap. Prowler was still watching them and the way the entire scene appeared was strange to War. "Looks like we've got trouble brewing in the corner and unless I'm reading this wrong, it's been set up to look like something it isn't.

He nodded towards the tables. "Prowler's about ready to make his move and with Glimmer gone, Merc gets to deal with the problem. You see Prowler's boy just sittin' there? He's waiting. Fuckers are like a bunch of damn chickens. One goes down, the rest peck their eyes out."

War looked around the room and spied Yo-Yo laughing with Boner. He walked up to her and whispered into her ear and she looked towards where Prowler sat and nodded.

She downed a shot of whiskey and rearranged her tits before walking over to Prowler's table, leaning over in front of him, blocking the sight of his whore and Merc. She grinned at the surprised man and grabbed his ponytail in her fist pulling his head back for a deep open mouthed kiss. She let go of his hair and twisted her body to sit on the table in front of him, stretching one leg to circle over his head and ended up sitting in front of him with her legs spread. Her bare pussy was right in front of him and she leaned over to grab his ears to bring his face where it would do her the most good.

"Your girl has been bragging that no man can eat a pussy as good as you can. I want to see if she's right. Come on, my pussy's been deprived while I tended bar tonight and she's ready to be licked and fucked." She laid back on her elbows with an arched brow and taunted him. "Unless you don't think you're up for the challenge. You like pussy, don't you?"

Race was almost laughing out loud as the men around the table with the beautiful woman began taunting the leader of the Scenic Heights chapter. They yelled and cat called, egging Prowler on and telling Yo-Yo that they could make her scream if he wasn't man enough for the job. She really got them going when she half sat up only using the obvious muscles of her stomach, pulled her shirt down below her beautiful tits, licked her finger and began circling a hard nipple. When she started twisting and pulling on her nipples, he dove in.

Bam laughed with the rest, but he was paying more attention to the other table. All taunting activities had stopped the minute Yo-Yo sat her beautiful ass in front of Prowler. Merc stood up and dumped the whore onto the floor without apology or even looking at her. Younger and Les stood up when he did, while Pauly stayed seated with three others. The three men started making their way to the barracks and Bam followed them at a distance.

Race watched the room and had to remember to tell the brothers that he was proud of them. Their numbers were still low, but it was a start, and this way the club could be choosy when it came to bringing in members.

The three main women that belonged to the club were still young enough and pretty enough that they kept the brothers happy. There were a few hangarounds that liked the idea of fucking a biker a few times a month. Those women came for one thing and the brothers gave them what they came for. The ones that used to come to the old club were a problem for him. Most had been so used and abused that they knew no other lifestyle, and Race had no idea how to deal with them. Yo-Yo and Goody had threatened to cut his dick off if he followed through with his plan to ban the older whores from being admitted into the gates.

Yo-Yo had flat told him. "You all are a bunch of selfish fuckers. Those women lost their youth and self respect being used by this club, they deserve better than that from you selfish motherfuckers. Town people call them biker trash and they aren't welcome in the bars in town either. Where do you expect them to go? Wolfman and his rules might have been bullshit, but pussy was pussy to him, so you'd better rethink your plans if you want to enjoy a good life."

She hadn't been so easy going when he reminded her that he was the president and deserved her respect.

"Really? You want me to respect you? I've got news for you asshole, you want my respect, you can fuckin' earn it."

Goody had said the same thing. "You still have some old scooter tramps in the club and they did the dirty with those women for years. Are you planning to turn them away too?"

He'd been having a discussion with the two women on an early morning run day, and once he told them to get rid of the old whores, that was when he caught hell. When he got back from the ride, they had another talk.

"All right, I can see your side of the problem and I agree to a point." He'd pointed his finger at Yo-Yo since she'd been the most vocal in defense of the older women. "You make damn sure they get checked for STD's and keep 'em clean when they're here. I won't tolerate a bunch of worn out whore's begging for a bump from anyone willing to fuck them."

He knew that at least four of the aging passarounds were being stashed at the club somewhere, but he hadn't bothered to ask or seek out their whereabouts either. As long as they came into the club clean and smelling like they took a shower, he had no problems with them. They'd actually made the transition from one place to the other easier for everyone. They did the major cleanup around the place and even washed a brother's clothes and sheets if the man asked and was willing to pay a few dollars for the convenience of someone else doing the chore.

The slaves that Wolfman had working in the shed had been loaded up in the support van and taken three counties away to drop them off in front of a rehab hospital. The poor bastards were so fried that only a few of them remembered what day of the week it was, but Race wanted nothing to tie the Breed with the five people, so they had to go. No bleeding hearts argued with him about that which wasn't a surprise.

The room was emptying out, with the only real concentration of men still watching Prowler do his damndest to make a good showing in front of his brothers, Yo-Yo wasn't making it easy on him either. She recruited two men to suck her nipples while she taunted Prowler to, "Make me scream."

Race couldn't help himself, nor could several of the other men, when the whore Prowler had brought to the party got up from the floor, and attacked his bent head while he was eating Yo-Yo's pussy. He laughed until tears leaked from the corner of his eyes.

"Motherfucker, licking that slut's cunt, what the fuck? You said I'd get anything I wanted if I made nice with Merc and his boys, and the minute I do what you say, you're fucking eating another woman's pussy? Fuck you cocksucker, I'm gonna kill you." How the bony woman pulled Prowler and his chair backwards on top of her with both of them hitting the floor, Race could only wonder. The whore was out cold from the hard wooden floor meeting with her head when they went down.

Prowler rolled over to get to his hands and feet. Yo-Yo sat up and hopped off of the table and walked away. Her mood had been interrupted and she went stalking other game for the orgasm she'd been cheated out of. The small crowd wandered off since the show was over.

Prowler's men left the room with their leader carrying the woman over his shoulder. He tried to leave her where she landed, but War stepped in and told him, "take your bag with you, we're not responsible for her, you are." The evil look that the man shot at War only made the big man smile. "If there's a problem man, we can deal with it here and now. I've got no issue with tearing your head off and shoving it up Merc's ass. Be happy that Race might have missed the play you two were trying to make while you are our guests. He has a serious hate for disloyalty in the Breed, no matter what corner it comes from."

Prowler tried to heave the prone body from the floor to his shoulder, but she was dead weight and her limbs kept getting in his way. His booted foot connected with her belly and she moaned and curled into a fetal position.

War shook his head and leaned over to heave the woman into the air at arm's length and flopped her over the smaller man's shoulder. "There you go, all nice and stable. By the way, you want to tell me what happened to Glimmer? As in what did you and those ass lickers do with the body?"

He got another scowl for his question and he shrugged before Prowler moved away with his woman. He stumbled a little when he heard War's question, but kept going once he got his balance.

War commented, "I imagine Race won't take kindly to finding the Brother's body after you all are gone, people might lose confidence in the leadership."

This time there was no mistaking the grin and look of triumph on the asshole's face, War had all the proof he needed to complete his own plan.

*****

Race came into the freezing warehouse knowing what waited for him. Bam and Flats, along with three of the other chapter Presidents were there as well as War and Billy. There were five men hanging by their feet from the old ropes and pulley system that tracked the entire length of the huge building. Shingles and boards were missing in spots, and the freezing rain could be seen and felt as it blew through the spots that were in need of repair.

Billy was filling the buckets with water again and lining them up for the next round of questioning. Race saw that the ropes holding the men captive were wrapped tight around the boot tops of the men to suspend them without creating skin damage. When the bodies were found in a day or two, there would be no questions about how they died. For once, the weather was working for the captors and Race grinned as he approached Prowler's dangling form.

"I hear that War asked you nice to tell him what you did with Glimmer. I don't personally give a fuck how you killed him, he's no friend of mine any more than you are, but I don't like surprises." He nodded to Bam and watched as the brother doused Prowler with a bucket of cold water. Given that all five men were already soaked and shivering, the water might have felt warm to his captive for a few minutes, but that would soon change.

"So, maybe you didn't like the way War asked you for the information. Let me see if I can do a better job of communicating my wishes."

Race began pummeling Prowler in the belly. It didn't take long for the bastard to toss up what was in his stomach and Race backed away just as the liquid began to spew from Prowler's mouth.

Turning his attention to Merc, Race could see that the man wasn't about to tell him anything, this one was a fuckin' psycho. "Not gonna bother with you, I don't like spinning my wheels, so I'll see you in hell." His steel-toed boot connected with the side of Merc's head three times and it was over. The blank eyes held no life and the brain matter that decorated Race's boot tip began to freeze.

Les pissed his pants when he saw his friend's brains and blood trickling from the hole in his skull, so Race turned his attention to him.

"You want to save me the trouble of dealing the same way with you? Start talking."

Through shivering teeth Les spilled his guts. "Prowler and Merc planned to rule Kentucky, you know, share. Gonna have a sweet set up in the middle ground and get the products out from a central location. Glimmer had his own agenda."

The men standing around them nodded in understanding and shot Prowler looks of dislike. Grinder, the president of the Conner Arkansas group, stepped up and stood next to Race.

"I'm thinking you're not gonna like the answer to where they stashed ole' Glimmer and that's why they seem reluctant to talk." He pulled a tool from his front pocket and Race grinned.

He waved the man forward towards the prisoners. "Have at it. I'm not greedy, but save Prowler for me, if you don't mind. If there's one thing I can't stand it's a god damned backstabber."

It wasn't all he wanted the bastard for. He needed to show these men that he would take care of business with every attention to detail. Prowler would be his poster boy for the rest of the men in the room. They'd realize that he would gut them, just as he planned to do with the fucker hanging in the middle still coughing and trying to breathe. He eyed the other two Presidents and made a decision.

"You see those two on the end? They're fair game for you, no retaliation, no prejudice, if you feel like showing them what happens to those that abuse the privilege of being a member of the Breed. If not, you can walk away with no problem."

Grinder set to work on Prowler's vice and from the screams the man gurgled out, and the number of teeth that were piled on the floor under his head, they heard that Glimmer's body was dumped in the men's room in the bar in town.

Race sent Billy to tell Mambo and go with him in the van to pick the body up. He also gave orders to make sure there was nothing left for the women to find the next day.

Once he heard what they had done, War ripped open the shirts of Prowler and Grinder's victim. He pulled his blade from the side of his boot and traced the tip from Drake's lower abdomen to his neck. "You have a problem here, motherfucker. You see, both of those women at that Bar in town happen to be special to me. One of them in particular. Call me old school, but I protect what I consider mine." He stabbed the blade deep into the soft tissue of the fucker's underbelly and proceeded to saw the blade sideways through muscle and guts. The stench was unbelievable, but it didn't stop the rage inside of War as he thought of River finding a dead body in the bar. The poor woman would be hysterical and he'd be damn lucky if she spoke to him again, or any brother for that matter.

"You might as well enjoy this if you can, especially when your guts start falling into your face, it's gonna be a lot more painful before I let you die." The fucker was silently screaming as War cut straight down from underbelly to the bottom of his ribcage. The intestines and organs flopped out and down his chest, but the man was unresponsive. He might be breathing, but he was as good as dead. War stepped back and reached into one of the buckets of icy water to rinse the gore from his blade, wiped it on his pant leg and re-sheathed it. Then he picked up the bucket and slowly poured the water over the open space now visible for all to see.

Race glared at War, the fucker had taken his idea and improved on it with the T cut, but still. Fuck. How was he supposed to...? *Fuck it.* He was the Prez, he could do what he damned well felt like doing. He took his own blade and approached Prowler. "You hear what happens when you plan a coup like you did? We live by honor, loyalty, trust, our code, fuck with one, you fucked with all of us. You knew the consequences and you lost." He stabbed the tip of his blade in each of Prowler's eyes and slit his throat as he hung screaming.

The last two men to die were luckier than the rest. Stabs to the heart and one to the carotid artery were the worst of their wounds, but the men that did the deed hadn't balked or tried to get out of the task before them. They knew it was a test and they knew that their days were numbered if they hadn't stepped up. Personal feelings aside, this was business and they treated it as such. Race and the three presidents went back to the clubhouse to warm up and make appearances in case they had been missed.

Bam had left the warehouse and enlisted Pete and Flats to help with the bikes. They removed all personal affects and the VIN plates from the nicest three Scoots, and Glimmer's bagger, before they replaced them with similar, but definitely inferior bikes, and loaded the steel up on a flatbed with ten gallons of gasoline and kerosene. The tragic accident would be a devastating loss to the Breed when they were found at the bottom of the drop off. It could take weeks to determine identities and causes of death. In the inclement weather, rescue efforts would be hindered, but they had to hurry if they wanted to make it appear to be a legitimate accident.

Four men stood catching their breath as they looked down the snow covered icy drop off. They were waiting for Bam to jerk on the rope for them to haul his big ass back up the steep incline. He was arranging the bodies in the right spots so they would get maximum exposure to the fire already licking through Prowler's Kerosene soaked body and clothing. The full gas tanks with the open petcocks would catch soon too, so he made sure to arrange the bodies close to the bikes before soaking them with the gasoline. He shook his head and said a brief prayer before grabbing the plastic jugs in one hand and tugging on the rope that would take him to the top. The fire was starting to gain intensity and he didn't want to be holding flammable containers in his hand if a spark should fly his way.

They had a hell of a time turning the truck and trailer around on the snow covered, icy road, but they had to leave because of the light from the fire blazing in the inky darkness. If any citizens were out and about tonight, the light would be seen and reported, and they wanted to be gone way before anyone showed up to investigate.

CHAPTER 11

It was a good thing that Mondays were slow and that they didn't normally open the bar until four in the afternoon. River was dragging ass and Maisie wasn't her usual cheerful self either. The drive to the bar was treacherous and unless the snow stopped soon, they might be forced to stay in the back room for the night. By nine that night, Mother Nature had dropped another six inches of snow and the bar was empty of patrons.

River made the decision to close the place. "We've been dead all night and the few drinks that people bought won't pay the electric bill for the day. Let's close up shop and try to make it home so we will have some extra time to pack and be gone by first light if we want to be."

Maisie looked around the empty room. "I'm going to miss it here. It's the first place that I've been in that I felt like a normal woman, you know? After all the years with Wolfman and then he started giving me to his brothers and friends, I felt like garbage. Like it wouldn't matter if I died, because I was already dead. A few of the brothers were nice to me, but they felt sorry for me and I knew it."

She looked at River and shrugged. "Did I tell you that there was a young girl that Sea brought into the club last Christmas? She was only fifteen years old, and they..." She couldn't go on talking about what had been done to the girl. "I saw them and I remembered how I felt when it first happened to me. I tried to get her to leave, but she was scared. I found her in the shower with her wrists slit and that was the day I decided to start killing them, the men. I got all of them but Zero, and he died with Wolfman, so my ghosts are in harmony about what I've done."

She stood up and lifted the chair to place on the table top. "I never actually considered that I would get away with it. I thought that one of them would wake up and kill me when they realized what I was doing. It wouldn't have mattered at the time. Now I have a future and I'm not sure what to do with it. Crazy, right?"

River knew the feeling, she hadn't actually believed that she would succeed in gaining revenge for the deaths of her family members either. She had prepared for the real possibility that she would be killed when they realized that she was the one causing the club so many problems. The two of them had more in common than helping each other rid the earth of the vermin that caused so much misery. They'd been ready to die to do it.

As Maisie said, "I have a future, and no idea what to do with it." The words played on her mind as they began shutting the place down and locking the doors. River pulled the folded envelope from her pocket just before they left through the back door and set it on the cash register. It was her resignation and an apology all in one. She hadn't elaborated on her reason for leaving, only that, *it is time for me to go home.* She thanked Darnell and Dena, and wished them every success in selling the property.

River was thankful for the four wheel drive in her old truck. She found that as long as she took it no faster than ten miles an hour, the roads could be negotiated since her truck was higher off the ground than a car would be.

By the time they got to the rented trailer, her hands were shaking from gripping the steering wheel. She had to tell Maisie, "Unless the plows come through and the weather clears up, we might be here for another day or two." Even exiting the truck was dangerous because of the accumulated ice on the short driveway in front of the trailer. She fell on her ass as she walked around the hood of the truck and sat for a minute in the snow before grabbing the bumper and hauling herself back to a standing position. The only thing that saved her from falling on the metal steps was her grip on the door handle and the railing.

When she came out of the shower Maisie grinned at her and handed her a cup of herbal tea that she'd just brewed. "Not a big deal, two years ago we got an ice storm followed by a snow storm, followed by another ice storm, all in the space of two weeks. No one went anywhere. Trust me, you get a few dozen bikers snowed inside and they get crazier than normal. As long as we have heat and electric, we'll be fine."

*****

Mambo met Race before noon the next morning. What he had to say wasn't good news for the club. "I checked the place over thoroughly, if there's a dead guy there, I have no idea where he could be and I even checked the coolers under the counter."

Race was pissed at himself for not making sure that Les had been telling the truth. "Fuck, now we have a problem. They could have dropped the damn body anywhere. Did we check the woods around the property?" He hated the idea of dealing with Pauly and the two men that were left from Prowler's group. He actually liked Pauly from previous dealings with the man, it would be a shame to have to force the information from him. He'd do it, but he wouldn't like it.

Mambo looked like he had something more than a dead Prez on his mind. "Ok, let's hear it, what's got you all twitchy?"

War and Bam walked in the door and Mambo sighed. He walked over to the door and locked it behind the two of them and returned to where Race sat scowling. He took the crushed envelope from his pocket and handed it to him and began pacing the room. War and Bam watched the restless brother, then turned their attention to Race. His scowl was worse than a few seconds ago.

"Oh fuckin' hell no. Not just no, hell fuckin' no. That little bitch thinks she's running off to who the fuck knows where when she's got my goddamned guts in knots?" He shook his head and tossed the note across the table towards War. "Our bird is flying the coop and if this note is right, she left already."

He looked at Mambo who was staring out of the window. "What's got you in a mood?" Mambo either wasn't paying attention to his question, or he hadn't heard him. "Mambo, what's got your nuts in a vice? I know what's got me pissed, but if you tell me that little bitch has you twisted up like she has me and War, I swear I'll beat her ass until she can't twitch it at any one else."

Mambo looked confused for a minute and shook his head. "You mean River? No it's not her, she's too bitchy for me, you know that, or should." He glanced at the other men in the room and shrugged. "I think Maisie went with her. She's nowhere at the bar where she was using the backroom to bunk down. Her stuff's gone. She wouldn't come back here unless she had nowhere else to go." He stopped moving long enough to look Race in the eye.

"I've been thinking about buying the Double D and maybe making Maisie my woman. She's gotten some confidence since the fire and I was letting her get used to being independent for a little while, before I planned to ask her to be with me. She seemed to like me well enough, but if she's gone with River, I can't blame her. I can't blame either one of them for leaving. River got to see Wolfman fall, and Maisie was set free to live her life. Who am I to stop her from leaving?"

War's mind caught the reference to River and Wolfman. "Hang on a sec, what did you mean about River? She wanted Wolf dead?" He snagged a chair and Mambo and Bam followed his lead and sat down with Race, who was looking lost and confused at the conversation. He nodded at Mambo and said, "Spill, all of it. We can figure this out and decide what to do to get them back."

Mambo was looking at Bam and shook his head. "Not until I know what he's doing here." He pointed his finger at Bam and asked him, "What's your reason for being here? One day you show up and say you're from Timbuk-fuckin'-tu, and suddenly you're the Sergeant At Arms. Wofly and the boys are toast, but you kept a low profile for a couple of years now. My question stands. Who the fuck are you and what are you doing with us?"

Bam reached for his wallet while War watched his hand pull the chain from the top of his pocket, pulling the wallet out and into his grasp. He opened the thick leather and took his driver's license from the plastic cover to toss across the table to Race.

"My name is Justin Warren, I did come from the January group, and fuck you too. The club is getting too many alpha bastards and I figured if I was going to have to fight every damned night, I might as well fight with people that deserved a good ass whippin'. Wolfy and his bastard boys came through a couple of years back. I was away, fuckin a whore two states over at the time. When they left, my sister was left beaten and in a fuckin' wheelchair. She was also pregnant and had two STD's to go with it. The baby was still born and my sister got a hold of a bottle of painkillers. Three days after I laid her in the ground, I headed out." I've been trying to find a way to isolate Wolf and his pack. Every fuckin' time I'd get a few of them together, something happened, someone showed up." He tossed his hands up and they dropped into his lap. "It was like those motherfucker's had a damned angel watching over them.

"I was close enough, I could have pulled those fuckers out of the line of the explosion, but I watched them burn and laughed as those fucks melted. I laughed in Wolf's face while he laid there still smoking. He saw me and I told him why I hated him, and the bastard had no idea who I was talking about." He looked directly at Mambo. "How can a man not know when he rapes a young girl and him and his friends beat on her until her back was broken, and walk away, forgetting her face? He was a fuckin' rabid animal, a goddamned cancer. And I wish it had been me to kill him."

Mambo looked to Race and got the nod. He looked at War, and after a few seconds, War nodded his head too.

"A couple of years ago, we had a brother they called Tuck. He was good with numbers and I think he did the books for the club before he got dead. He was a big ol 'boy, damn near as tall as War. Tuck was a good guy, kept a low profile, but you could count on him, you know what I mean?" He looked at Race and shook his head. "One day Tuck saw Wolf doing something that would get him killed if it got out. The kid didn't know that everyone already knew that Wolf and Zero were fuck buddies, and I don't mean they shared a woman. Rumor had it the kid walked into the room when Wolf was on his knees sucking cock." He blew out his breath and swallowed, remembering the kid's lifeless eyes.

"My Uncle Darnell and me got him wrapped up in plastic and called the phone number tatted on his ankle. It was his sister and her name was River. I knew who she was the minute I heard the name at the bar. Hell, she bleached her hair, but her eyebrows are the same color as his hair was and the eyes are the same too. It took us all fuckin' day in the van and we met her that night, left his body in the bed of her truck."

He was silent for a minute. "I know she had something to do with Wolf's death, I just don't know how." He remembered, "My Uncle spilled the beans that we knew who her brother was, so she's probably afraid I'd rat her out to the club. I ended up telling her the part about finding his body and admitted that Uncle and me were the ones to return the body to her. She took it well, surprisingly well.

"She was more than cheerful the day after the fire when I went to check on things. I didn't call her on it, I'd been trying to think of a way to kill the fucker myself."

War finally got his answers from the evening of the fire. He knew who had helped Maisie. The puzzle fit so well and he had been so blinded by her size that he felt like a dumbass, but that didn't stop him from bursting out in laughter and continuing laughing until he was wiping his face with his hand trying to stop the loud noise he was making. Every time he looked up and saw the way the men looked at him, he would start sniggering, and try to speak, but the laughter kept coming.

Race threw an empty beer bottle at his head and he barely got his hand up in time to deflect the thing from hitting his head. It took some doing but he finally gained control of himself.

"I got it. I know how she did it and when I see her again, I am going to bust that fancy little ass of hers again, this time I might kiss it all better when

I'm done." He held his hand up to stop the questions that came at him.

"Picture it, a man is murdered for seeing something he could never un-see. His little sister gets the body and somehow knows who killed her brother. Now let's assume that little sister shows up in the town where the murderer lives and starts a campaign of slowly taking out some of Wolfy's biggest supporters. That drain cleaner was probably the same stuff they used at the bar. The bastards deserved to die, but our girl probably lured them with that sweet ass of hers, got them drunk or slipped them something to make them pass out, all she had to do was make sure they dropped where she left the bodies." He shook his head in admiration.

"Let's say our girl decides to up the ante, she gets tired of picking them off one at a time, so she recruits someone to help her. Let's say someone no one would suspect agreed to be her partner. Someone that has reason to hate the Breed, or Wolf and his cronies as much as our girl does? Remember the mysterious fire at the shed?" Nods came from the three men at the table beside him, and he continued.

"Say our girl rigs the propane tank and has her companion ready with a remote device to set the thing off while everything is chaotic. Who would think it was a certain abused, over used and ignored woman who never said boo to anyone that hit the detonator? I saw Gum – Maisie with the thing in her hand, I knew she set it off, but I thought one of you had her working with them." He grinned and

103

looked at his companions. "Say they stick around long enough to avert suspicion from them and then they vanish. No one would think that two little women could cause so many deaths, or mayhem." His head was still shaking back and forth in wonder. "I'm, hell, the genius of the plan worked to help all of us, and I'm in fuckin' awe. I don't know how they did it exactly, but now that I think about it. It fits."

The room was silent as the men considered War's theory. There were questions and they all hashed them out, being interrupted twice by knocks on the heavy wooden door, and the people on the other side of the door were told to, "Fuck off and hold your shit for a few" for their trouble.

Race concluded their meeting with, "They're probably afraid that if by some remote means, we figured out they were involved, that we would retaliate and hurt them. Hell, I want to pin a fuckin' medal on them." He looked at Mambo and Bam.

"You two find out where they are, stop them and bring them here. It's time to deal with the wild women and I'll be damned, but I'll wear my hand out on River's ass if she gives you any trouble. Just don't tell them why you're bringing them back, let them worry for a while. Mambo, if you want Maisie, she's yours. Keep her out of trouble, my man."

CHAPTER 12

The electric held out for the night and into noon the next day before it quit completely. They had everything but their blankets and coats loaded into the bed of the truck within an hour and decided to take their chances on the roads.

River came in one last time as Maisie put the last of the perishables into a bag to toss into the trash on their way out of the park. River left the key to the trailer on the counter along with the week's rent. The landlord knew she planned to leave at the end of the week, so he would find the key and money when he came on Friday. She looked at her companion.

"Let's get this show on the road. If we're careful, we should be in Illinois by tomorrow and then Kansas the next day. We aren't on a schedule, so if the weather turns bad on the way, we can find a hotel for a night or two. Heck, if we want to take a detour and go see the museums in Chicago, we can do that too. I went to Brookfield Zoo one time, it was great."

Maisie nodded and tossed the trash on top of the canvas bed covering before she climbed into the passenger side of the truck.

They were quiet as the first hundred miles were put behind them. The roads had been shitty and many of the roads were plowed with only a small one track to drive through, but they made it to the interstate in one piece and were soon putting distance between the past and their futures.

Maisie never learned to drive a car let alone a four by four, so River decided that she had had enough driving for the day by six thirty that night. "I know we planned to be further by tonight, but my shoulders are killing me from being so tensed up trying to keep the truck on the road. Let's find a hotel that has a hot tub and a restaurant that serves something alcoholic and has little umbrellas sticking out of the top of the glass. What do you say?"

Her companion grinned. "I've never stayed in a hotel to tell you the truth. I went to summer camp when I was a kid, but I've never been in a hot tub or had a drink that didn't come out of a plastic cup or a bottle. I'd love to see how the other half live, even for the night. Are you sure? I don't have money to pay for anything much. I used my pay from the bar to buy clothes and pay for my eye and teeth. I'm sorry I can't contribute more than maybe fifty dollars."

River decided to tell the girl at least part of the truth about herself. "Look, I'm not worried about the money. The truth is, I've got some money and can get my hands on more if I need it. Remind me to tell you about my life sometime soon. I don't like talking about it, but the truth of the matter is that we could spend a month or two in a hotel that's better than anything we'll find on this trip. When I told you that you can go to school or be whatever you want, I wasn't lying. As my best friend, I'll help you financially and get you set up wherever you want to go."

She didn't like to let people know that she had money in a trust fund from the death of her parents. The insurance that Tuck had finally gotten was a ridiculous amount of money that had been sitting in the bank for years now. At least helping Maisie find a good life was something that she could feel good about. She might lose her new best and only friend by helping her, but the money would be put to a good cause.

The bar and vehicles from Mr. McCormick's estate were hers too. And she got the payments for the bar every month from the people who were under contract with a balloon payment at the end of the year. She had been counting on the people to surrender the place when she came back, but if they were doing well and still wanted to buy the place, she'd be out of a home of her own.

Yeah, poor little River, you hated that place, you have time, money and a life to discover in the big world, quit pissing and moaning about your pitiful life.

She pulled into a chain hotel and had to relax her fingers from the steering wheel before she could turn the key off and unbuckle her seatbelt.

After checking in, the women went to the back of the truck to remove their suitcases, and it took a few minutes to get the key in the lock. She had to wipe the ice and road dirt from the slot and the back of the canvas cover. It was already dark, but Maisie held her cell phone open to provide light while River fumbled with the key and icy stuff.

A van drove in behind them and they heard doors opening and closing, but were too busy to pay attention. The women were grabbed from behind. Big hands covered their mouths and when they left their mouths, the women had both tried to scream, so rags were stuffed into their mouths and tied behind their heads. Pillowcases were pushed over their heads and they found themselves taped together back to back lying in the back of the van. Doors slammed and they could feel the vehicle backing out and then forward.

River was scared, who had kidnapped them and what did they want? If they planned to rob them, all they had to do was go through her purse and pockets. They didn't need to take them like this. Were they planning to rape and kill them? Maybe leave their bodies on the side of the road? Every possible threat that she could think of that could happen to two women by themselves could be done to them crossed her mind and she resolved to save her energy for when they stopped. Her size lured a lot of people into underestimating her abilities. Hopefully she'd get the chance to escape.

*****

Pauly was waiting for Race to show up, he had Fat Boy and Orin with him, they weren't the brightest of men, but they made good soldiers and that's why Prowler brought them along. Pauly was still in the dark as to why he'd been told to mount up when they were leaving, but he did as he was told at the time and regretted having been in eyesight of Prowler on their way out of the door. Now Prowler and Drake were gone, their sleds had vanished with them and Pauly was left wondering why they'd been left behind. The whore was still sleeping it off in the barracks and he thanked God for small blessings. Prowler had called her Precious, but lately she'd answered to anything. As long as a man had a needle and was willing to give her a bump, she would do anything he wanted. He didn't want her riding with him once they were back on the road. He wouldn't give her a fuckin' aspirin, let alone 'H', fuck that. He saw Race and War coming down the steps and waited until they had cups of the crap that passed for coffee around the place, before walking over to make inquiries.

"Hey Race, I need to make some inquiries if you get the time." Race nodded to the chair between him and War. Since it was the only other chair at the table. His companions retired to the bar to try their hands at flirting with Goody and Queenie.

He sat and gathered his thoughts before asking, "Prowler and Drake must have left last night or early this morning, didn't say a word to any of us. I wondered if he wore out his welcome or if you know why he'd leave in the middle of the fuckin' night?" He got a negative shake of Race's head and sat back in his chair. *What the fuck?*

War spoke up from his left. "After that little deal with his whore, Yo-Yo ended up daring him to watch while Merc ate her cunt, but he left with his woman. I'll ask Bam and Billy. Hey, there's Flats, hang on a minute, maybe he knows." He waved at the bartender and watched as he walked over to the table.

"What's up?" When War asked him about Prowler, Flats laughed and shook his head. "Those fuckers got into an argument and decided to go for some kind of dare. I didn't get what the bet was about, but they were talking about the better biker. Last I seen of them they hit the door and planned to ride on the ice. Crazy fucks for sure. The damn snow was coming down so bad I spent the night on one of the couches in the meeting room. Why do you ask?"

Race thanked him and Flats walked off towards the bathrooms in the back hallway.

"Well, at least we know they couldn't have gone far last night, the snow is on top of an inch of ice. Even drunk they wouldn't risk their scoots in this shitty weather." Race grimaced at the taste of the coffee. "Damned swill, who the fuck made the coffee today?"

*****

Pauly nodded. "I agree, thing is, their sleds are gone, me and the brothers looked all around outside. No sign of them anywhere."

War tilted back in his chair balancing on two legs for a minute before standing up and telling them he'd ask around.

He came back ten minutes later looking concerned. "We might have a problem. Merc and those two assholes' with him, are gone. I checked the room they were in, and all of their shit is still there. I don't like to think it, but they might have run into problems while they were riding." He looked at Race. "As soon as the plow trucks go through, we'll start searching for them. My truck is good in snow and mud, but it don't handle worth a shit on ice, so when the sun comes out, I'll take a couple of guys out to look for them."

Once Pauly left the room, War told Race, "We need to get some snowmobiles if this kinda weather is going to keep up like this. I wasn't joking about the truck on ice. Four wheel drive isn't any better than any other vehicle on ice for Christ sake."

The men went about their business for the next few hours. The only bright spot of the morning was the message on Race's phone. It was a text from Bam. *"We got the packages. Mambo is driving River's truck since she's kinda tied up at the moment. The roads are for shit, but we should roll in around midnight, barring any unforeseen problems."*

War took Pauly and Banjo out to look for the missing bikers and Race got a list of things they needed to get from town for the kitchens. He told the visitors that they needed to pony up some cash to help feed them. "We weren't expecting to feed you fuckers indefinitely, so if you want to eat, open your damn wallets."

He got in his new pick-up and wasn't surprised to find the roads slick, but the chains that the brothers put on the back tires helped him navigate to town with no problems. He loaded the grocery cart with food and stashed it in the bed of his truck in black plastic garbage bags to keep them from getting wet from the snow. He decided to walk over to the video store and look for something to entertain them for the next day or two. They didn't have cable or satellite TV at the club yet, so it was three channels of shit, or rent DVD's.

He got three action adventure movies and then went into the small room in the back where Georgia kept the porn. When he saw the additional merchandise for sale, he grinned and took his time deciding what he wanted to buy. He came out of the room with an armload of porn to rent and his selections to purchase outright.

Georgia wanted to talk. "Business has been slow this week, I almost didn't bother coming in today." She rang up the rental fees and the merchandise, reaching under the counter to pick up and then toss a white bottle into the bag. "That's a freebee, I appreciate your business."

Race grinned. "Thanks baby, one of these days you need to drive out to the Clubhouse and we can show you how well we treat friends of the Breed." He winked at the older woman and she grinned back.

"I might just do that sometime real soon."

Race was still smiling as he drove back to the winery. Ole' Georgia was an attractive woman for her age that he estimated to be fifty or so, and he went through the older brother's in his mind to see if he could match her up with any of them, thinking about Flats or maybe Rascal. They were older men, no families, and no bad habits that he knew about. He'd have to send one or both of them back with the movies. Georgia might appreciate that.

He had to pull over for several emergency vehicles to creep past his truck and almost got stuck when he hugged the shoulder of the road. If he didn't have those chains on the tires, he'd be digging for an hour to clear the deep snow away from his drive tire. The more he thought about War's suggestion, the better he liked it.

Snowmobiles would be a welcome mode of transport for winter days like this.

Back at the winery, he parked the truck and grabbed the bag of videos and the personal things he bought, telling Benny and Hinder to unload the truck. They were a couple of the prospects that had stayed on after the renovations. They appeared to be good guys, but you never know a man's worth until he's tested, and so far, there hadn't been any significant tests.

He left the videos on the table under the sixty inch flat screen in the meeting room and took the rest up to his room. Dumping the bag's contents on the bed, he grinned as he began to open the packages and put fresh batteries in the toys that used them. The bottle that Georgia gave him was toy cleaner, and he decided to go ahead and wipe them down, just in case they needed it. It had been a few years since he played with a woman like he planned to do with little River, just knowing that she would soon be cuffed and at his mercy made his dick hard. He'd even decided what to do about War. They shared women all of the time, why not share River? That way if something happened to one of them, she would still be protected and have a man to turn to when she needed him. The solution was perfect. He hoped War felt the same way.

CHAPTER 13

River woke up when the door opened next to her head. Maisie wiggled at her back and she hoped they would allow them to use a bathroom because it was getting to be an emergency. The tape binding them together was sliced and she was dragged by someone pulling her body to the opening of the door. A man's voice told her to stand up and she put her feet down to the ground. She almost fell down, but after a few wobbly attempts she got her balance back and walked with the person holding onto her arm. She heard a woman's muffled scream and turned fast, she forgot that she couldn't see, and that she was being urged to continue on their way. She stood still and refused to move until she felt a hard smack on her ass. It caused her to jump and squeak behind the gag in her mouth and she had to squeeze her muscles to keep from peeing her pants.

Lord, she was cold. She bounced up and down from her knees, hoping to hold her bladder from letting go, it was difficult with the way she was being pulled faster into a building that was warmer, and jerked into a room before someone grabbed her jeans unsnapped and the zipper was pulled down. She was embarrassed by having a stranger pull her pants down and pushing her down to sit on a toilet. She was so thankful that she relaxed her stomach and pelvic muscles, immediately feeling the liquid being released into the water below. She sat there continuing to pee long after she normally would have, but all she felt was relief during the process.

The wad of toilet paper wiping her was done in an impersonal manner and she thanked mercy for small favors.

She started to stand and was pushed back to continue sitting. One foot was raised and then the other as her shoes were removed from her feet and her pants stripped from her ankles. Her zippered hoodie was removed and the long-sleeved t-shirt was pulled over her head. The pillowcase over her head was held down by a hand around the front of her throat, and the slight pressure that the hand used, scared her so badly that the remaining liquid in her bladder gushed from her body without warning.

She hung her head in embarrassment as she heard a masculine chuckle. The sound of running water gave her reason to be concerned. Were they going to drown her? There was nothing she could do about the shivering that started as a hand pulled her to a standing position and unclipped her bra. Her breasts were lifted and the nipples pinched, before the hands stopped fondling her and led her to a shower stall. She could hear the water and feel the steam from the heated water wafting into the room.

She felt a hairy leg rub against hers as she stepped into the steamy enclosure, and squeaked, but when she tried to jerk back, the swat on her bare ass caused her to rethink her plan of running from the room.

A hand reached up under the hood covering her head and laid a soft cloth over her eyes. A hand went to her throat and the material on her head was removed. A scarf was being placed over the cloth on her eyes, *no it wasn't a scarf*, it was some kind of elastic cloth. She could feel the soft texture of the covering on her temples. It was tight enough to hold the lightweight cloth in place, but left her chin and most of her face bare. She couldn't see a thing, but this was better than that hood thing any day. The gag was removed and she worked her jaw to make sure it was still operational. When she felt the warm water on her body, she leaned into the water to take a mouthful, rinse her mouth and leaned down a bit to spit the water out. She repeated the action twice more and began to feel a little better.

The hands turning her were warm and masculine, and when those hands started rubbing a bar of soap over her skin, she attempted to back away. There was nowhere for her to go when she backed her ass into the cold tiled wall and the pinch on her nipple caused her to stand still. The hand putting pressure on the back of her neck urging her to bend at the waist kept pushing even after she was bent double. It wasn't until her ass was in the air and her head was between two hairy thighs, that the pressure stopped, and when she tried to raise her head, she got a hard slap on her ass.

Whoever had her sure liked smacking her ass and she wondered why they'd chosen her. Her ass wasn't small and muscular or particularly sexy. It was a fact of her life that she could lose twenty pounds and never miss it. Especially in her hips and thighs. This man had both cheeks in his hands and, oh my god, there's another one, there had to be another man in the shower with them. While the first one held the cheeks of her ass open to expose her slit completely, someone else was running soapy fingers up and down from clit to asshole, and she cringed.

"Stop that, I can wash myself." Her declaration earned her another slap on the cheek of her ass and a muffled, "Shut up, or the gag comes back."

She really attempted to get out of their hold when she felt a razor gliding over the lips of her pussy. The razor went away and by the time that big hand stopped smacking her ass, she was crying out loud and shaking. He re-soaped her slit and continued to shave every inch of her exposed sex, even into the crease of her ass. The shower head was directed on to the freshly shaved flesh and fingers ran up and down, to check for strays. It was the most embarrassing thing that she could remember ever happening to her and she couldn't stop her body from responding.

Her gasps and grunts did nothing to stop them from continuing their exploration of her bare body, and when a set of fingers slid through and discovered the wetness that she felt trickling out of her pussy, she heard a small laugh.

A long finger slid through the slick cream and into her pussy made her cry out, but it was the shock of feeling the second finger joining the first that made her stand still. Those fingers kept hitting on her hymen and she knew that he knew that she hadn't been with a man before. Especially when she heard him say, "Fuck, the little witch is a virgin."

The other man said, "You've got to be fuckin' kidding me." Both male voices groaned and she tensed up. She knew those voices.

"You sons-of-a-bitches, just wait until I get loose, I'll make you wish you'd never seen me before I'm done with you. You can't just kidnap a woman and drag her back home to molest her and…"

She was hauled from the shower and roughly towel dried, before being picked up and carried into another room and tossed on to a soft mattress. When she tried to crawl off the bed, she was hauled back to the middle and War told her to knock it off.

"I'll do more than give your fancy, little ass a few smacks River, I'll tie your ass down and Race and I will torment you for the rest of the day. We can tie you to the bed and leave you naked with the door unlocked, anyone could wander in here and see you like that. Maybe even decide that you need to be fucked by a stranger, after all, you'll be blindfolded, and you wouldn't know who was fucking you."

She wanted to work up a serious hate for the rat bastards, but truthfully, she didn't believe they'd do such a thing.

"Look, I'm sorry, but I don't have time for this. Why don't we sit down over drinks and talk? This kidnap thing is fun and games and all, but I told you no. I'm willing to let this kidnapping thing pass if you let me get up and put my clothes on. I'm not going to run, you have my truck and my stuff right?"

Race laughed. "Really? You think we'd drink anything that you had access to? Given your history with drain cleaners and propane bombs? Girl, you are the delusional one if you think we'd trust you within thirty feet of something we planned to ingest."

She couldn't believe that Race and War had figured it out. Fuck, she had reason to worry now. They thought she had been the one to poison their biker buddies, but she wasn't going to tell them that Maisie had been the one that did it. She was no rat. They could be speculating and fishing for a reaction from her.

She shook her head and said, "I don't have any idea what you mean. I never used drain cleaner to hurt anyone. I'm afraid your information is fucked up. I didn't do it, and unless you have proof, you kidnapped me for no reason."

War laughed and she didn't like the tone of that laugh at all. It made the hair on the back of her neck stand up and she opened her mouth to scream. There was time to take a deep breath before a hand covered her mouth and she felt warm breath at her neck. His voice promised punishment, and she should have been more frightened than she actually was. Instead the scent of his skin and the hairy leg pushing her thighs open made her pussy rejoice. The betraying bitch was soaking her thighs and ass.

"You've been a very bad girl, and we've decided that we like bad girls. We're gonna fuck you and you're gonna like it. When you give us hell, we're gonna spank that ass." He took the covering from her eyes and tossed it to the floor, then moving his attention towards her bare pussy. "Somehow I don't think you'll suffer being spanked as much as you should, so we'll have to get more creative in disciplining you." His big hands ran down her thighs to lay his thumbs on each side of her pussy.

Race sat next to her head and played with her hair for a moment before turning her face towards him, bending down to take her lips with his in a scorching hot kiss that left her gasping for air. "We'll discuss your transgressions later. In fact, I think you're about ready for your first lesson in pleasing two men at the same time."

She was shocked. "Two men? Wait, what do you mean two men? I can't do that."

War laughed and shook his head at her naiveté. He didn't bother to try and explain. His grin was directed at Race, who was frowning at her ignorance. *Ha! Let that smug bastard explain it to her.* He began kissing the inside of her thighs, enjoying the textures of her tender flesh. To his way of thinking, the best way to learn something was to experience it, and he planned for River to experience a great deal today. Her pretty little pussy was luring his mouth with that lovely trickle of cream he could see glistening on her flesh, and he wasted no time in settling down for a nice long session of eating her virginal pussy. The thought of being the first to pop her cherry had his dick harder than ever, but tasting her pleasure, *oh yeah*, he was going to make their girl scream.

River couldn't believe this was happening. Not only had they figured out that she had something to do with the fire, but they thought she was guilty of everything that happened to the club members, and they still planned to keep her. This time they didn't give her the choice between them. They'd already decided to share her.

The touch of War's mouth on her clit made her shiver. The feel of his tongue licking her pussy lips and stabbing into the entrance of her body, made her moan. She wanted more, but Race pulled a handful of her hair and turned her face towards where she was face to head with his cock tapping on her lip. She looked up and he grinned.

"I know you saw people in the main room sucking and fucking, so you know what I want you to do. You can start by licking my dick and giving it a few kisses. Once you feel what you're dealing with, open your mouth and suck my cock." He tapped her on the lip again. "No teeth darlin'. If you bite me, I won't bother to use much lube when I fuck your ass and I don't think you would like a dry ass-fucking. I'll use enough lube so my cock is easy to slide in, but you need to trust me when I say, you want me to get liberal with the stuff. Now give it a kiss and let me see your sexy lips wrapped around my cock."

She could see that he wasn't going to be put off. His eyes were narrowed and when she stuck out her tongue and gave the head of his cock a tentative lick, he licked his bottom lip and his hand began rubbing the back of her head with a slight pressure urging her to continue with what she started.

His murmurs' of "*Oh yeah, like that*," and the low tone of his voice directing her actions kept her attention divided between hearing and seeing his pleasure while she was receiving the most amazing pleasure that she'd ever enjoyed. War kept nibbling and licking, she couldn't stop her own moans even with the thick meat of Race's cock between her lips, even when she took him as deep into the back of her throat that she could get him. She raised her hips to get more of the pleasure from the talented lips and tongue as they explored her pussy and clit. His finger penetrated at the same time that he sealed his lips around her clit and sucked strongly. She screamed around the cock in her mouth as the first orgasm that she was experiencing in a non-self-induced way took her thoughts and body over. The clench and release of her inner muscles on his tongue amped her pleasure and she screamed around his cock as she came. The cock in her mouth slid further into her throat cutting off the scream, as she tried to breathe with the thickness cutting off her air supply.

The silky texture of the flesh covering the hard muscle made it easy for her to slide her head up and down on his cock, enjoying the sounds that she was causing Race to make. Feeling his pulse through his cock was a thrill for some reason, and knowing that the longer and deeper that she kept him into her mouth made the throb of his heartbeat speed up and she wanted to see how fast she could actually make the pulse jump. She sucked him in and out faster and thought she was taking more of him each down stroke. He was groaning almost nonstop.

When War removed his lips from her pussy, she planted her feet on the mattress and raised her hips wanting to lure him back into continuing the pleasure he had given her clenching pussy. The feeling of something blunt and smooth was gratifying. As it came deeper inside, she began to pant. She felt her body stretching and suddenly she screamed as the thing slammed down and making her feel as if she was ripped apart.

While she screamed, the cock in her mouth slid down and deep into her throat, cutting off her scream. She felt the jerk of Race's hips and the way his cock jumped in her throat as he came while she struggled for breath. Her hands found his thigh and an arm and she sank her nails into his flesh, even as his cock began retreating enough for her to take in more air. War hadn't moved once he entered her so deep and she was thankful that he'd given her time to adjust her hips and relax from the sharp pain of his invasion. His voice distracted her from the discomfort, and she felt her heart go all mushy when he praised her.

"You're so fuckin' tight and I can still taste you on my tongue. Nothing, nothing better than you like this. Shit, I'm coming and I haven't even, oh God…"

She felt him swell and suddenly she felt the spurts of his cum with each hard jerk of his hips. The heated liquid flooded her and soothed the remaining sting from his invasion. His head dropped onto her chest and he took a nipple into his mouth to suck while his heartbeat slowed and his breathing returned to normal. His cock slowly retreated from her body and she giggled when it finally popped out.

Why she thought it was funny was beyond her comprehension, but the giggles kept coming until Race leaned over and kissed them from her lips. She didn't know that there were tears trailing down her cheeks even as his thumbs wiped them away while he calmed her with his lips on hers.

"It will be easier the next time darlin', we'll take care of you and make sure that you are enjoying us as much as we enjoy you. You did real good for your first time, you know. Thank you." Race kissed her again then got up and headed for the bathroom.

War stayed in his position and leaned over for a kiss that was every bit as potent as Race's had been, but held tenderness too. "Thank you, I've never had a virgin before, and I promise that the next time will be better for you."

When Race came back into the room, he had a towel and a soaked washcloth in his hands, and War moved from between her legs to give Race room to clean her up. She tried to take the washcloth, but he gave her a narrow eyed look and began wiping her pussy clean from the small amount of blood leaking from her entrance. The towel absorbed the excess water and he patted her dry. "There, all ready for later when we've had a while to recoup and catch our breath."

River had no idea what the protocol for after sex was. She sat up and immediately needed to go to the bathroom to pee. War smiled when she dangled her feet from the mattress trying to find the floor with her toes. She levered herself on her hands placed on the mattress and sort of hopped off of the bed and both men laughed.

She put her hands on her hips and turned to give them a piece of her mind, but the way they looked at her, it was a look that she couldn't describe even to herself. If she didn't know better, she might think they actually loved her. She shook her head and frowned at them, before turning and walking into the bathroom to take care of her bladder. She wondered where they went from there.

CHAPTER 14

River was asleep when they went downstairs, they'd put her though her paces for the first time. They'd slept on each side of her small body for a couple of hours, but decided to allow her to sleep for a few more hours as they knew she would need the rest.

Pauly and his boys were still drinking and War went over to their table when he saw the condition the three men were in. They'd "discovered" the wreckage yesterday and had been detained by the cops while the rescue workers went down to look for survivors in the tangled mess of metal and burnt flesh. The fact that Pauly hurled his guts out on the side of the road as they hauled bodies up and over the drop off, had been excused.

Franklin, a cop friend of the club, stood by his supervisor and a state cop while they asked questions. The answers that the bikers gave satisfied the cops well enough, especially since the victims were all out of town types. Locals knew about the drop off, and given the probability that the men had been drinking, combined with the snow falling at a rapid rate to hide the ice beneath the snow made it a tragic accident and War made all of the appropriate sad comments.

"We had no idea that they'd left last night, I could have warned them not to come this way if I'd known they planned to go for a ride."

The cops looked sympathetic, but the state cop was smirking as he told War that there appeared to be one body separate from the others that hadn't been burned. He'd been asked to stay and wait for the body to be hauled up, because the cops wanted him to try to identify the man. When they finally pulled the board up with Glimmer's body on it, War knew that his look of puzzlement was real. How in the fuck had the son-of-a-bitch gotten down there?

Mr. State Cop asked, "Can you identify this man so we know who he is?"

War and Pauly and the other two nodded their heads, even though Pauly began swallowing in an effort to stop himself from hurling again.

War said, "Yeah, his road name is Glimmer, he's been visiting from Kentucky. I suspect the boys down there are the guys he brought with him and the other two are more than likely Prowler and Drake. Fuck, this is a blow for the club." He'd shaken his head in sympathy for Pauly. "Man, I don't know what to say. I know they're your boys, but at least you can stick around to escort the bodies' home, depending on how long the state keeps the corpses. We'll give Prowler an escort fit for a club Prez." He laid his hand on Pauly's shoulder and gave him a squeeze. "This was supposed to be a celebration and it's turned into a damned tragedy."

He'd been frozen by the time the bodies and bikes had been pulled up over the edge, the bikers had gone over the drop off to assist in collecting the bikes to speed up the recovery. It had been a long, damned process. It didn't help when Orin found an intact hand and chased Fat Boy around the spot pretending it was a Zombie hand trying to grab him.

Pauly saw what was happening and a rescue worker took the hand from Orin with a grimace, but it was too late for Pauly. Fat Boy had to be hauled up the side with a passed out Pauly over his shoulder. Another rescue worker finally woke Orin from the blow that Fat Boy gave him upside his jaw. War wanted to laugh at the men, but his muscles were screaming from helping to pull Fat Boy and his burden up and over the edge.

War swore that the next time they had business like this to deal with that Race could handle it. National President or not, his happy ass could deal with some of the dirty work too.

Race walked over to the bar and listened to Goody and Queenie complain about the lame fucks that they'd dealt with overnight, and Yo-Yo came down the hallway slower than her usual breakneck speed. When she neared him, he noticed the way she was moving and asked her if she was hurt.

He walked towards her and she held out her hand to ward him off. "I'm all right. I got a little more than I asked for is all. When Bam gets in a mood, well, let's just say that he made his point. I'll be ok in a while." She noticed his frown, and she laid her hand on his arm after taking a quick look towards the long hallway. "Don't say anything or do anything. I asked for what I got, it's not all his fault for giving it to me. Bam and me have an understanding and I, well, you know how I like to challenge a man. I picked the right man for the job. It'll work out." She shook her head and smiled. "I've been around this club since my mother died back in '99. Bam and me go way back to when I was a snot nosed kid that thought she ran the men of the club. Puberty was a bitch and I was the curious sort you might say. He never forgave me for that."

It wasn't the first time they'd had words, but it was the most effective meeting between them. She wasn't about to confess that she was having a problem because she'd said some harsh things to the man she'd loved for years, but could never seem to get her words and actions to sync up. He'd proven to her what she'd believed since the first time he called her a whore was still true. To be honest, the first time had been ten years before and that was when he called her a slut. Tonight she'd been upgraded to Whore. She'd taunted him and he'd stepped up to give her, well she didn't want to think about what he'd done. There was no way he would touch her again and the knowledge made her want to cry.

If Race pushed her for an answer, she would walk out. No one but Bam and her would ever know what they'd done, even if she knew the memory would haunt her nights for years to come. She did her best to stand straight and smile with her usual friendliness.

Hearing Race say, "I'm here if you want to talk, or need someone to adjust his attitude." Made her smile turn grim, but she nodded her head as she carefully walked past the big guy. The club was home, and she was thankful that she had some of the best people alive to call on if she ever needed them. The problem was hers and she was living with the choices she'd made. Maybe it was time for her to move on. She'd grown up here, all kids left home at one time or the other, didn't they?

*****

River woke up alone in the big bed. She looked around and found her clothing from last evening scattered around the bathroom, and when she saw her face in the mirror, she saw nothing changed. Shouldn't she look as confused and, well, something after spending the night with the two men who were determined to have her? Now she knew what the fuss was about she should look as different as she felt.

She'd masturbated plenty of times over the years. Enjoying a mind blowing orgasm while a man was licking and sucking on her pussy, well, that was altogether a different kind of pleasure. Her jaw was a little stiff, but by the time she rinsed her mouth and washed up, there was just a little discomfort inside but nothing that would have warranted the blood stains that she saw on the comforter. She put the damp clothing on to cover herself before snooping around the room. She picked up a pair of jeans from the floor and could tell the pockets held items in them, so she reached into the front pocket and pulled out her truck keys. She clutched them in her hand and stuffed them into her pocket, before digging through the rest of the pockets in both pair of jeans belonging to the men.

She pulled the comforter from the bed and tossed it into the corner along with the men's clothes that were littered around the rooms. War really seemed to get off on the fact that she'd been virginal, and she'd be damned if she was going to feed his ego by allowing him to gloat over the evidence that would be plain to see when he walked back into the room. Why they'd brought her back was a mystery to her. Maybe they didn't like being turned down and decided to double up because they figured she'd be more inclined to pick one of them if they both had her at the same time. Whatever their fucked up reasoning, now they'd had her and left her. She checked the door and found that it was unlocked. So the threat of leaving her for anyone to walk in and have wasn't just a threat?

Knowing that they didn't bother to make sure no one could just walk in and find her asleep, and therefore fair game, hurt. She had hoped for more. Why, she had no clue. It would have been nice to at least hear a few words of affection, a declaration of love would have been laughable from either of the men. *Wouldn't it have been?* She sat for long minutes on the bed and came to the conclusion that she had to leave. Race told her he wanted her to do what the women in the common room did and she couldn't deny that she had done exactly what he asked of her. She would let them pull her fingernails out before admitting to liking the way he trembled in her mouth and under her fingertips while she sucked him off. The thing was, she didn't want to be another passaround like the women he wanted her to act like. She wasn't wired to mindlessly lay herself out on a table and allow herself to be used like that. She wanted to be loved.

She could hear the muffled sound of vehicles starting up and she ran to the dirty window to look outside. She couldn't tell who was leaving, but one of the vehicles was that hopped up four by four that she remembered from days ago. There was a pile of snow under the window and she hoped that it wasn't just covered up plow mounds covered in an inch or two of snow, or her plan to jump from the window would result in possible broken bones. A snowdrift wasn't a big deal as far as she was concerned.

As soon as she didn't see anyone milling around the area, she slid the window up and took the time to remove the screen, before climbing out on the sill and taking a deep breath. *You can do this.* She launched herself out and her body dropped faster than she planned, but she almost cried when she felt her legs sink into the deep pile of snow without encountering any jarring connection with ice blocks. She crawled out of the snow and didn't bother to take the time to brush the snow off of her shoulders. Her truck was in the parking lot, and she saw that her purse and jacket were in the passenger seat. All she had to do was unlock the door and climb inside.

She was scared that she would be stopped before she could leave the property, but she ducked down in the seat when she saw two people emerge from the front doors of the building. It was Mambo and, damned if it wasn't Maisie, holding his arm while he leaned down and said something to make the tiny woman smile. River shook her head. At least Maisie looked like she finally might get her happily ever after. Over the time River had known the woman, Mambo's name had repeatedly come up in conversation. Lucky girl, it appeared that he held some affection for her if the protective way he bent over her smaller body to block the wind was any indication.

She waited until they'd gotten into his truck and turned towards town, before she started the Durango and eased towards the gates. They'd been left open and for the first time that she could remember, there were no prospects in a car or standing around. She drove through the gates and began to breathe again. Instead of heading west like she had the last time she left, she headed east. She kept driving through back roads and small towns until she needed gas, then looked for a station that was busy. Fueling up in the cold was not her idea of a good time, but the faster she left the area, the more distance she put between her and the bikers, the better off she felt she'd be. She used the facilities, grabbed a couple of candy bars and bottles of water when she went inside to pay cash for her purchases. The lure of the cappuccino machine was too much to resist, as she picked up several sugar packets and two small bottles of energy drinks. When she got in the truck, she poured one of the small bottles of energy booster stuff into the hot drink and several packets of sugar. The boost of triple caffeine and sugar would keep her alert for the rest of the night so she could get the miles expanded between the bikers and her ultimate destination. Thanking her own stars for not telling Maisie their ultimate destination, she started the truck and continued on her way.

Checking the rearview mirror constantly kept her nerves on edge. It wasn't until she turned south to double back when she got to Alabama that she relaxed. She could take her time and drive through Texas. It wasn't like she had to be anywhere in particular on a certain day.

They probably aren't looking for you either. They got what they wanted and left her asleep and vulnerable hadn't they? The niggling thoughts of betrayal refused to leave her brain. How could they have sex with her, mind blowing sex, and leave her alone like that? One thing they proved to her was that she wanted them and now that she'd had them, how was she supposed to forget how it felt to fall asleep between the two of them? *Men are such uncaring bastards. Fuck them, I'm not a damned toy to be played with and left on her own until they decide that they want to play again.*

CHAPTER 15

Race had no sooner walked away from the bar to go to the kitchen to try and scare something up to eat when his cell buzzed to get his attention. It was the Sheriff's office and they were needed to come in to give their statements about the biker's that were recovered from the drop off. He retraced his steps and found War hauling Pauly up from the chair to help the man to the barracks to sleep the drinking binge caused by the traumatic find of several bodies and bikes.

Race yelled at Ben to take over the task and War looked puzzled, but handed the slender biker off to the prospect.

They gathered Flats, Bam and Ben when he returned from dropping Pauly onto a bunk. On the way outside, War called out to Billy and Pete to come with them. They took both War's and Race's trucks filled with bikers to give statements about the last time anyone saw the deceased men. The sooner everyone gave statements, the sooner the case would be closed, so Race decided to get it over with.

Before they left, Race called Goody over to him as the rest of the men gathered their coats and walked out into the sunny cold air. "We left River upstairs in my room. When she comes down, will you show her where the food is and if she wants to bitch about last night, I'd appreciate it if you could calm her down. I don't want to leave her like this, but we need to get this out of the way to keep the heat from showing up at our door later on."

She grinned. "You two fucked River? The little woman from the bar? That's so cool. I can get her outfitted for working the floor." She bit a long, acrylic nail while she thought. "Ok, I might need to get creative for clothing for her, if I remember right, she is pretty short but curvy. Right?"

Race counted to ten before answering her. *Fuck.* "Look, she isn't working the bar, not tonight, not ever. You can have Joey and Elton get her stuff from the back of that White Durango in the lot. They can leave her stuff outside of my room. They are not to open that door for any reason. Warn them that I won't be nice to anyone that bother's River. She's mine and War's woman. Pass that around if you don't mind, I don't want to have to hurt someone because they didn't know better than to move in on our property."

If he hadn't been in such a hurry, he might have laughed at the look on Goody's face when she heard him claiming River publicly. "Thanks, we'll be back in a few hours, so I'd appreciate it if you could make her feel welcome."

Her head nodding up and down was good enough for him, and he hurried outside to get the show on the road. The sun was shining bright and the snow and ice were melting at a rapid pace. The puddles of slushy shit were a pain, but knowing that the weather would warm up a little was a welcome thought. Winter in southern Ohio was mild compared to some of the places he'd been to in his travels. Snow didn't come down in foot deep measurements, it usually came in a few inches at a time. They normally got plenty of black ice on the roads and cold wind that would cut through a man, so a warm up into the thirties would be welcome.

Walking into the sheriff's office made the hair on his arms stand up. War hated the cops, all of them. Even the ones that he tolerated. Donny the cop wasn't a bad guy, too bad he was sworn loyalty to the other side. He might have made a good brother. The state boy was sitting in on the questions and listened to each biker recount his whereabouts the night that they knew the accidents had occurred. When it was his turn, the local boy left the room and War wondered what the fuck they wanted. He wasn't good with set ups and he smelled a skunk in front of him.

"Look, they were drinking, and when men get together, we challenge each other, you know that, so why the cozy chat set up?"

The cop stared at the file in his fingers and opened the cover. "I have no doubt that the men were tanked up when they went over that embankment. That's not what I want to discuss. Word on the street is that you boys are trying to buy businesses and front as legitimate business people. I want to get the story straight from the source. The fire at the old Clubhouse was convenient for you and Race, and now the death of two of the Breed's chapter Presidents seem to be a bit fortuitous for your plans wouldn't you say?"

This asshole was closer to the truth than was healthy, but War shook his head. "Are you fuckin' kidding me? That fire took out over fifteen people and the reason that the National Prez got toasted was because of his arrogance. Several of us, myself included, yelled for him to get the fuck away and he ignored our warnings for them to move. Short of running through the flames, there was nothing I could do. Race was on the other side of the building with me because we saw the women that belong to the club just standing around about twenty feet from the fire. We grabbed them and kept them moving before the tank blew." He cocked his head sideways and scowled. "You know all of this already. Why don't you just tell me what you want, and I can tell you what you want to know, or I can even get up and leave this building."

The boy in blue sighed. "Okay, were you aware that Prowler, also known as Dean Capozio, was related to the Vinchy Group?"

War shrugged and began to stand. "I don't know what you are trying to say here. I've never heard of the Vinchy Group. What does that have to do with Prowler's death?"

"We think that the deaths of your biker brothers might not have been an accident. We think that somehow, some way, the Breed has gotten in trouble with the hierarchy of the Vichy family. If you think of the logic, our assumption is reasonable. Sit down and I'll tell you what we are thinking."

This line of thought was fascinating and as long as the Breed wasn't under scrutiny, fuck yes he'd agree that the Easter bunny had laid in wait for the chance to get even with the Breed for rabbit hunting and eating his relatives.

"We had a deal going with Wolfman and one of his associates, a man that he called Zero. He had been giving us information on the Vichy representatives that certain men in your organization obtained high grade blow from a source in South America, to sell in the urban areas of several large cities. Wolfman was dead before we got the information about the next shipment. We thought that three years of hard work went to hell when it was confirmed that Wolfman was expired before we could get anything. We knew that your friend Prowler was one of the contacts, so it was a fairly simple thing to go back over the tapes and find out that Prowler and company were the 'go to' people to obtain the drug of their choice."

He spread out several gory photographs for War to see. "We figure that Wolfman double crossed them, never actually believing that they could reach out and touch him. The club presidents were just fodder, but fodder that could implicate the killers. They had to go."

War wasn't sure what to say, "Well damn, how did I miss seeing this happening? We should bring Race in here for this discussion."

The cop shook his head. "No need, my partner has informed him by now. You guys need to keep your heads down, at least for a week or two. If they believe that more of you were involved, it could get nasty quick. The only reason I'm telling you this is because my supervisor said that since our contacts are dead, the second incident might have been accidental, but it all adds up to be an almost unbelievable coincidence. Just watch your back, man."

War stood up and nodded. "I assume this information comes with a price tag?"

The cop shook his head. "No price tag. It would be nice if you let us know if you hear anything from someone in the Vichy group though. They are going to want that delivery line to stay open, and my money says they will be looking for contact."

The logic was amazing, considering that the Vichy family could have made the move, but hadn't.

"I know this information will fall in the unbelievable category, but for what it's worth, Race and me have made it known that we want the Breed to move out of the pharmaceutical business. It might cause a small faction to disagree with our thoughts. I know that no one has contacted me, and if they'd contacted him, I would know about it. So if they did cause all of the carnage, then they killed their last mule and might as well cut their losses."

He left the cop sitting there when he walked out of the room. Once Race and the rest of the boys met them out by the trucks, War waited until everyone but he and Race had taken seats in the vehicles to talk privately.

"We got a rat, but the cop handed us a golden ticket, a get out of suspicion card. Did you ever hear about a possible Mob connection?"

Race was shaking his head and looking around the parking lot. He turned his back to the building and said, "Later, but they're fishing, you must have got the Good Cop side of things and I got the hard assed motherfucker that tried to make me confess to something I had no part in doing. The brother's gave their statements, then lawyered up when the pissants started tossing around accusations. So fuck them, we're done here, and if they want to talk to any of us again, they can do it through the suits."

War considered what Race just told him. "You know something? I think their rat was one of the boys that died in that unfortunate accident. Do you remember how Drake glared at us like telling us to fuck ourselves? I'd bet a few hundred that he decided to act the psycho so you'd do him outright. I never saw him acting fucked in the head like that before, he knew he was meeting the reaper, probably decided to do it in one piece."

Race thought about it and nodded his head. "Could be, we'll discuss it later. Right now, I think I'm hungry for a taste of River. I've been thinking about her all morning and I'm thinking that we need to explain the situation. She needs to know that she's our property now, and I hated to leave it to Goody to spread the word. We need to take it to church, let the brothers know that she's ours, and see who objects to it. Not that I give a shit, not giving her up, but we have rules."

War agreed. "We should probably get her a gift or something, you know, to make it official to her. We should maybe stop in town while we're out and pick up something to give her when we get back to the club. She's likely to be pissed that we left her like that. Women like romantic shit. We should be able to find something."

They gave Bam the keys to Race's truck and the brothers piled into the double cab to return to the club. War and Race took his truck into town. It was a good opportunity for them to talk without ears possibly listening in to the conversation.

Race grinned. "I've got a few things for her already, did you know Georgia started selling sex toys?" War looked interested so he gave him a rundown of the things he'd purchased earlier. "I got two different sized butt plugs and some of those metal balls the Chinese used to give their ole' ladies when the men went off to war. Since I already have handcuffs, I bought some of those clamps for her tits and several bottles of lube. She's so fuckin' small, I don't want to hurt her, so I picked up plenty of the stuff in different flavors too.

"Seeing her juice sliding out after that few smacks on her ass about did me in. Our girl has a liking for having her ass spanked and I have a liking for smacking that ass, so she'll fit right in between you and me."

War nodded. "We need to make the quarters at the winery bigger if we plan to stay there for any length of time. You know how women are, they collect a bunch of crap and make a man happy to see the doilies and afghans on the furniture and shit. That building that sits out behind the warehouse? We might want to look into renovating that, structurally the place is sound, but it's gonna need a lot of work to make it into a home." He glanced at Race.

"We need to be sure that this is what we both want. River is a little bitch at times, but I don't want to see her get hurt. I'm ready to commit to the long haul with her and I actually like the idea of the two of us being there for her. I think about how fragile life can be at times, and I like the idea that she won't be left alone to fend for herself if something happens to me.

"Before you start ragging on me about love and shit, look at yourself. If you aren't ready for the relationship to stick, then you need to back off. As soon as I saw her, I've wanted her. I actually like her personality, fuck man, how many women do you know that would come after her brother's killer without back up and marginal skills? I got respect for the little witch."

Race nodded his head. "Yeah, I get you, and I get what you're saying. The thing is, I feel pretty much the same way about her that you do. She's right about one thing, we have a weird connection or some shit. I wouldn't think about sharing my women before. I'm not talking about the whores and passarounds, I mean *my* woman. Believe it or not I had the same thoughts about her not being alone if one of us died." He looked out of the side glass, checking the rearview mirror before continuing. "I can't bust you about the love and heart shit because I figured that out last week. Fuck man, when Les said that they left Glimmer in the bar, my brain clouded red, all I could think of was rushing over there to keep her from being upset when she found a dead biker. I was afraid that she'd be scared."

As they parked in the small lot of the mini mall, Race held his hand out to shake War's hand to seal the pact. "She's ours for the long haul."

War repeated his words with a grin. "For the long haul."

CHAPTER 16

River made it to western Kentucky by midnight. It was much warmer and no ice or snow decorated the greenery on either side of the road while she traveled along with the windows down and the radio cranked up. She followed a weathered sign that led to a small hotel off the highway to sleep for the night. She was tired and she was depressed, but she was proud of herself for taking her destiny into her own hands. As much as she wanted to be loved and love in return, she wasn't about to become just another slut in a long line of sluts for any man, or in this case men.

She turned her phone on just for a few minutes to see if they noticed that she was missing, or if they'd forgotten her already. Although she didn't recall ever telling them her cell number, they could have gotten it from Darnell and Dena, or even Maisie. There were twelve messages, and only two of them were not from the same number. The first was a message from the people purchasing the bar in Kansas. They were ready to finalize the sale of the bar and wanted to purchase the garage behind the place that she had the bikes and truck stored. Her personal things were in plastic bins sitting in the back of the truck and the cab.

The second call was from her lawyer telling her the same thing that the purchasers had already said. The third call was from Dena and she left a long winded thank you and wishing her luck in her travels.

The next nine calls started out with Maisie telling her about Mambo and the plans they were making to buy the bar. From that point on, Race and War demanded that she return, then they requested that she return. Threats of busting her ass, to tying her to their bed followed the demands. The last call was War's sexy voice asking her to call to let them know she got where she was going and to let them know that she was all right.

"I don't know what made you leave, we had to talk to the heat about the accident. When we got back, you were gone. Come on Shorty, you have more guts than this. A woman who came to town and almost single handedly gets her revenge on a bunch of bad asses isn't a gutless little girl who runs scared. Call one of us and let us know you are okay."

She made sure that she turned the phone off. She knew that they would be able to trace the phone by reporting it lost or stolen. As much as she hated to get rid of the expensive cell, she needed to buy a new one. After a few weeks, she might be able to use the phone again. War and Race would forget about her fairly quick as long as she stayed under the radar. She decided to stop at Wally World the next time she found one and buy a cheap pay as you Go phone.

She woke the owners of the hotel and apologized, but they seemed to take it in stride, as if being awakened at midnight by travelers on the dark country road was routine for them. The man was named Walter and his wife was Jupiter. The names certainly fit the two people who appeared to be hold out hippies from the nineteen sixties, and she thanked them for interrupting their night to assist her. She breathed deeply as she stepped back into the night air. The smell of burning pot was giving her a bit of a contact buzz in the short time she'd been talking to the couple, and she was glad to get out of the room.

Her room was spotlessly clean and the linens on the bed smelled as if they had just been changed. The small bathroom didn't have a tub, but the hot water was in plentiful supply, and she took her time allowing the steam relax her tension of the day away. For the first time in days, she touched herself, imagining War and Race were the ones doing the touching. Now that she knew how it felt to have a man's cock deep inside of her body, she wanted to imagine that War's thick cock was hers for the taking, but the lack of his big body made her fantasy empty. Even remembering Race and his demands for her to take his cock into her mouth was hard to do, but she could imagine their touch as she manipulated her clit and nipples into an orgasm. She cried out their names and was immediately brought back to the fact that she was alone, and would be for the foreseeable future.

Her pussy still pulsed and begged to be filled when she lay in the comfortable bed, so she pushed her fingers as deep as she could, and rubbed her clit with her thumb to finally achieve a full orgasm. It left her panting, but at least she would be able to sleep. She needed to get some rest, because tomorrow she would have to travel the highway to get to Kansas by Friday to finalize paperwork for the sale. She needed to find a spot to park the bikes and the Studebaker. Thinking about the bikes, she wondered what had happened to Tuck's bike. After all, technically it was now her bike. Not that she would recognize his scoot if she saw it. He'd never come back home once he'd left. All she remembered was that the bike was chopped and it was black.

Sleep clouded her mind and she snuggled into the warm coverlet.

*****

Ever since they'd returned from town armed with two white gold wedding bands, a bouquet of flowers, and found that their Shorty had left the premises, hell raged through the winery.

The men were renovating the building that they'd discussed as being an ideal solution for the situation with River. Whether or not they got her back, the place still needed attention and it helped to take their minds off of the woman that should be with them right now.

Race had been so mad that he put a reward out for the brother that found her. "I want to know where she went, and the man that brings me the information will get his pick of bikes in the warehouse." Three hopefuls had thought they spotted her in Indiana, but checking into the information and finding that the woman in question was nothing like River earned the brother reporting a beat down by Race or War.

She'd been gone for three weeks when they decided to work on the building, and pounding nails helped work the rage from their systems, but people still walked softly when the two big men were close.

War had begun tightening up security and threatened to rip the patch from a brother's cut if he was caught compromising the security of the place. A second offense would result in expulsion from the Breed for his lifetime, if he was lucky.

"Since no one admits to being assigned to the gate the day Shorty left, from now on, you stay until your replacement shows up. If you have a problem, you dumb fucks know how to use the cell phones on your hips, call the bar. The first man to challenge me will learn the hard way not too fuckin' compromise the security of the club a second time."

When the cops finally released the bodies of the six bikers, arrangements were made to cremate what little remained of them, including Glimmer's corpse. War made plans to escort the remains and personal effects back to the two clubs. Race decided at the last minute that he should go with them. Bam was left in charge even though he wasn't thrilled about the prospect.

Race had a talk with him. "Look, if you can't see your way clear to deal with the club at half capacity, then maybe you want to step down and we'll find someone else for the position. I'm not a fuckin' nursemaid, nut up or step aside. You know how important this ride is. We show that we respect the chapters, they show us what they're made of. War's going because he has family in Juanita. I can't leave the place without leadership so you are or you're not. Make up your mind here and fuckin' now."

Bam tightened his lips and nodded in agreement. Race was surprised when the man clasped his shoulder and told him, "Be safe, and watch your back, the club needs someone like you."

He nodded his head and went to pack his saddlebags.

CHAPTER 17

The sale went smoothly and River felt the tears falling as she picked up the last two boxes of her things that the new owners had collected from the bar and the apartment in the back of the building that she had lived in for the majority of her lifetime.

She rented a large storage unit to secure the truck and bikes, but she wouldn't be able to keep them in storage indefinitely. At least that was the case with the bikes. Hers would be kept, along with the Studebaker truck, but the antique bikes, well there was no way for her to ride them even if she had them customized. The '46 Indian and the elderly chopper were impossible for her to kick over the motors. The insurance agent had offered her a low ball price for both bikes. She wasn't stupid, even if he thought she was. The bikes were worth a small fortune if she wanted to put them on the market. Something made her think of Race and War whenever she looked at them.

She had been gone for three months and wondered if they ever thought of her. Every night and hundreds of times during the day, she carried their pictures in her mind. It was ridiculous and she needed to move on. This love stuff was for the birds. She finally made her decision about the bikes. Now she needed to find a direction for her life.

Friday morning she watched as the transport people loaded the two scoots into the trailer and secured them from falling with padded rails and nylon straps. It seemed right when she made her decision to send the bikes back to Ohio, but seeing them closed up in the back of that trailer saddened her. *At least you won't have them haunt you every time you see them*, and the bright red bows attached to the handlebars with a long zip strip were her way of saying goodbye to the memories of the two handsome bikers.

She was headed to Colorado. Instead of racking her brains to figure out what she wanted to do, she decided to travel around for a while and learn some of the things that she'd never done before. It was three days after the New Year's holiday and she'd gotten reservations at one of the ski lodges because she figured that she should at least be able to say she tried skiing. The rental unit for her possessions was moved to St. Louis, Missouri since the place was centrally located and she could access the unit at anytime if she decided to settle in one place.

She checked her old cell phone and teared up when she saw that they hadn't forgotten her existence. Each week she tortured herself by listening to their voices demanding that she return, and now, they just asked her to call and let someone know that she was all right.

Was she wrong? Would they have had everything they wanted from her and pass her down the pecking order of Breed Brothers? She'd asked herself the same questions over and over and always came to the conclusion that if they'd wanted a serious relationship they would have told her. If not told her, they could have woke her and told her they'd be back, but they hadn't and they left the door unlocked too. It was better this way, her heart would heal, she hoped.

She took a taxi to the airport, as the brochure said, it was time to have an adventure.

*****

Bam was summoned to the gate to vet a truck that the driver said he needed to make a delivery to Race and War. The burly driver looked tired, but he also was irritated.

"Look, I get paid by the mile, I don't get paid by the time, so just open the fuckin' gate so I can off load these beauties. I'll turn my rig around and get the fuck away from this crazy damn part of the country. I never seen so many 'tards driving hell for leather up and down the damn hills around here that you seem to have."

Bam shook his head. The driver was obviously an asshole, but then so was he. "Open the box so I can see what you got to deliver, then I'll decide."

The driver got out and opened the locks on the trailer doors, opened one side and gestured for Bam to enter the enclosed trailer. "You should 'a seen the woman that stood around making sure I secured them upright. Cute little thing, demanding, but she paid cash."

Bam wasn't paying much attention to the man talking, he was running his fingertips over the beautiful bikes, then checked the cards and saw both War and Race's names on the envelopes. "Did you say a mouthy blonde sent them?"

The driver grumbled, "Yes sir, told me she'd gut me if something happened along the way. Truth to be told, I like the chopper, but I like the Indian too.

It's not often that I get to transport such beautiful machines." That told Bam all he needed to know and he came from the back of the box grinning.

He stepped aside and waved to the brother at the gate. "Go ahead, I'll help you off load them. You'll still have time to make it through the hills before dark."

Two days later, Race and the brothers rolled through the gates, and everyone seemed to be in a decent mood, so Bam waited until they dismounted their bikes and shook the tired muscles out before he broached the subject.

"Hey bro, nice to see everyone is back and in one piece. You need to come with me for a minute if you can drag your tired asses over to the shed, there's something there that you want to see."

War stomped past him and Race and Bam followed close behind.

War yanked the door open and stopped all movement. He could see them as plain as dirt, but looked backwards to Bam. "What the fuck is this?" And, "if they're hot I don't care. We can paint them." He walked over to the chopper and admired the old fashioned flames running along the tank, and the apes with leather fronds hanging down from the ends. The leather bags behind the seat and the drag bar, fuck, if the bike had been a woman he'd be balls deep in her right now. "Race, check it out, damn, these are some beautiful pieces of art."

Race was having a similar experience with the Indian. "That's my baby, or you will be soon." He turned to ask Bam who the old scoot belonged to, but the man had left him and War with the bikes.

"I'll be a motherfucker, but I want this baby." He noticed the bow and card right off, but until he turned the envelope over, he didn't comprehend what Bam had been trying to tell them. He held the card in his hand and told War to look at the one on the Chopper.

"It looks like they're gifts, I wonder what the cost will be and who gets paid." The title for the bike was the first thing he pulled from the envelope and he choked when he read the name of the former owner of the bike. "I'll be a son-of-... War, did you see?" War was waving the title to the chopper at him and sat on his ass on the floor close to where Race stood.

The men were reading the note that was included with War's card.

Hi guys,

I inherited the bikes from the man that kept me and my brother alive for years. I'm gifting them to the two of you. Every time I looked at them, I thought of you. I know that you will take good care of them. I couldn't bear to sell them, they had to go to someone that would appreciate the scoots for what they are, not just for the dollars they'd bring. I hope you learn to love them as much as the former owner loved them. If I'm wrong, then sell them and enjoy the cash. I won't know, so it will be your choice.

I hope all is well with you and the club, and please tell Maisie that I haven't figured it out yet, but I'm working on it.

Take care, River.

Race sat down beside his friend. "Now what do we do? Did you see who these bikes belonged to? Fuckin' Dallas McCormick. That man was a legend. I've only seen one other bike with that metal tag on it, and that thing was fuckin' cherry. I'll bet if you look at the riser on that chopper, you'll see the same tag. He didn't build the Indian, it's been customized, so it must be a personal transport, but that chopper has his hallmarks in every line."

War opened and closed his mouth a couple of times before he got his scrambled brains to think. "I noticed. I also noticed the name on the title, no wonder we've had shit for luck finding her little ass. R.T. McCormick. We've been searching for River Tucker. No one said a damn thing about that last name, the old man must've adopted her."

He sat thinking, and shook his head as he stared at the bike that he planned to ride the tires off of. "I thought Dallas McCormick died years ago. Hell, I half thought that the man was just an overblown legend. Looking at the chopper, I can see that he earned the rep. She must care or she wouldn't have just given us the scoots. Fuck, look at them for Christ sake. Who gives away things like that?"

Race nodded in agreement. "Yeah, the only person that would give away something like them is a person with money to burn, or someone that actually cares for and respects the recipient. Fuck, just...*fuck*. There's gotta be some way for us to find her. I haven't wanted a fuck with any of the women. It's almost embarrassing. Even Goody couldn't get me off, and you know she's got a mouth that can suck a man dry and leave him with a smile on his face."

War took up the complaining. "Yeah, and waking up with your dick as hard as possible because the little witch won't leave your brain. I wake up hard and," he shook his head, "I've taken more fucking showers in the past few months than I took in the last six months before she came on the radar. This shit has to end. We need to find her and bring her back. I'm for tying her to the fuckin' bed until she's too damned pregnant to leave."

Race laughed at War's wishful thinking. "I've been thinking about that. The more I think about it, the more I think we need to lock her up with us and make her fall in love with you and me. We can be lovable, right? At least I hope so. She killed for revenge for her brother's murder, can you imagine how fierce she'd be if she loved us?"

They went to the clubhouse and continued to rack their brains for ways and means to find River and bring her back.

Bam was grinning when they walked into the room, and War stomped toward the kitchen to grab some eats, his damned stomach thought his throat had been slit and was making grumbling noises for the past hour or so. When he walked back into the bar, he saw Race tapping on a computer. He walked over and sat down across the table from Yo-Yo, who was looking all smug and shit.

"What's up?" He took a big bite of the ham and Swiss cheese sandwich while he waited for an answer to his question.

Race answered while he was reading something on the screen, and Yo-Yo pouted for a second before she was back to smiling.

"It seems our Bam decided that he would get the license plate number and company name from the delivery guy. Yo-Yo has been busy with this new toy of hers that she has been learning to play with. She suggested that I learn to surf the net. I found the company, it's out of Kansas City. I typed R. T. McCormick, Kansas, and got an address in a town called Betwixt. I looked up the address in the records of the town and found out it's called Betwixt and Between. It's a bar." He looked up at War and continued. "I had Yo-Yo get the phone number for the place and it's recently changed hands. River left town right after the sale papers were finalized, and she moved her stuff to Missouri. Now I'm trying to find her in Missouri." He kept tapping away at the keyboard of the little computer.

"Nothing comes up under River Tucker McCormick or River Tucker." His fist hit the table causing everyone but War to jump. "She's in so much shit when I get my hands on her." He stood and walked out of the room.

Yo-Yo shook her head at his back. "You two assholes have it bad. So I'll keep digging until I find her. If I have to look in every damn state of the union, I'll find her." She looked up from the keyboard. "When I find her and you get her back, don't fuck it up. You men are such dumbasses that it's a miracle you can remember to pull your dicks out of your pants to take a damned piss."

CHAPTER 18

Colorado had been interesting. She hated falling down time after time on her rented skis. The instructor had been a handsome twenty–two-year-old with a toothpaste smile and thick, wavy, blonde hair. She had enjoyed most of the week that she'd been there, and Jordan had been entertaining. His kiss had been nice, and he had a line of compliments a mile long. He hadn't been upset when she told him no.

"I'm sorry Jordan. I came here to forget men and I like you, but, I guess I'm not ready for another heartbreaker to come through my life right now." He had smiled when she'd called him a heartbreaker. His ego showed plainly that he was used to women falling over themselves to get his attention, but the compliment gave him a boost and he wasn't very upset. Within minutes of her rejection, she saw him chatting up a ski bunny in a white jumpsuit and a nineteen sixties hairstyle. Looking closer at the woman's face, she could see that the lady had quite a few years over and above River's age, so his defection made sense. Mr. handsome was a gigolo or had a serious eyesight problem.

Now she was sitting in the airport waiting for her suitcase to show up on the carousel so she could take a taxi to the storage unit. She figured that she could drive the Studebaker for a few days until she replaced the truck that she'd sold when she moved everything to Missouri.

She knew where she wanted to be, but how to make it work was beyond her. She'd given herself time to heal. The months had not been easy to be alone, but now she could safely say that she had come to terms with her transgressions and made peace with the demons inside of her that made her think negatively about herself. The loneliness was crushing at times, but she gave herself permission to finally grieve. She'd sat in the darkness on a pile of snow, and had a long talk with River Tucker McCormick.

The tears had frozen on her cheeks, but once the heart to heart was finished, and she'd gone to her room and gone to sleep. She knew the next morning that she'd done what she needed to do. She'd made peace within herself. The heaviness weighing her soul was gone. She couldn't change the past, and helping Wolfman on his journey to hell had been the right thing to do. The warmth she had felt at the time of her self-examination sealed that niggle of guilt for causing so many deaths. From what she knew of the victims of the fire, the ones trapped in the basement that she didn't even know existed were close to death already. According to Maisie, they were in the basement because they were hiding from the law for felonies, or drugs had already taken their lives leaving empty, raving lunatics or drunken zombies with a thirst for their drug of choice instead of brains.

It was too late for her to feel comfortable wandering around in a deserted storage facility, so she opted to stay the night in the hotel across town near enough to the storage units that she could walk over and get the truck.

The next morning, after a bagel and coffee in the small restaurant at the hotel, she hiked across the road and punched the code to open the gate into the small silver box. She walked through the gate and over to her unit. The key was in her hand and she was ready to open the unit when she got a creepy feeling. She looked around and saw a large man at the corner of the line of buildings. He was talking on a cell phone and staring at her.

Fuck, she didn't have her gun or even her boot knives. Everything was inside of the storage units. The bike was in the companion room. Her guns and riding gear were with the bike. The truck had taken up most of the large room. It had several large tubs of personal stuff in the bed, and she hoped there was enough room in the small side to stack the plastic totes. She turned back and hurried to open the door and stepped inside. She stood inside the door in confusion. The room was empty. The sea green Studebaker was gone and so were her possessions. Panic was leeching in and she shook as she inserted the key into the side door to access the smaller room.

Someone pounded on the door, and she knew it had to be the fat guy that she'd seen earlier. She yelled through the door an unfriendly, "what?"

The door cracked open and an envelope was tossed inside before the door was quickly shut. She approached the white letter sized packet, and bent down to look closer before she picked it up. Her name was on the sealed envelope. She leaned

against the door and ran her finger under the flap.
There was a single sheet of paper inside, and she
knew what happened to her truck from reading the
single line.

River,
We have your truck and boxes of stuff. You
know where we are.

They hadn't signed the note, but she knew who
wrote it. She wondered how they'd found her, but
that didn't matter to her right this minute. She
grinned, they hadn't forgotten her. She did a little
dance drumming her feet on the concrete floor and
turned in a circle. War and Race were holding her
truck and possessions hostage and she began to
laugh. They'd found a way to force her to decide,
but the solution had already been in her heart. Now
all she had to do was decide if she wanted to go
back as a winner or a whipped puppy. The choices
didn't sit well, so she picked up the keys she'd
dropped and opened the side door.

Ha! They'd missed her bike. The shiny red and
chrome still shined for her pleasure when she pulled
the cover off of it and she wasted no time lacing on
her boots and gearing up. She still had to stop back
at the hotel and get her clothes, but she had a place
to be now. The knowledge kept the smile on her
face. Hearing the engine of her bike made her
happy. It was going to be a long road, but in the
end, the reward could outweigh the sore butt and
shoulders from the ride.

The creepy man was nowhere to be seen and she hoped that he was gone. The men wouldn't be expecting her to ride up on a bike. They would expect her to be in a cage, and knowing that they had a lot to learn about her made her smile in anticipation. Knowing that they were in for a surprise made her feel justified in teaching them that she wasn't just another helpless woman, depending on men.

*****

She rolled into town at three thirty in the afternoon, four days after she received the ransom note from the guys. She stopped by the bar, and walked inside with her helmet under her arm and surprised Maisie who was clearing a large table in the middle of the room. She tapped the little woman on the shoulder and stood back waiting for her to recognize her.

Maisie turned with a smile, and stood stock still for a second, until she realized that River was the person who'd tapped her on the shoulder. She grinned and squealed an ear piercing noise that made River's ears ring.

"River, *Ohmygodit'sgoodtoseeyou.*" She left the buss tray on the table and hugged her tight. "I missed you so much, you have no idea how much I wished that you were around in the past few months. Where've you been hiding? Race and War grilled me and I didn't know where you were. I'm so happy that you've come back."

River knew that the reason Maisie was staring at her was due to the fact that she now had her natural dark blonde hair instead of the short bleached do she'd worn while she was there before. She didn't say anything about the leather outerwear, but she had raised an eyebrow when she looked her up and down at arm's length.

"You look good, better than good, actually. You've lost weight. I'm just gaining weight like crazy, but by the time I've stopped gaining I will lose ten pounds or more, so I don't mind gaining the extra pounds." She patted her belly, and River starred at her hand and comprehension dawned.

"You're pregnant?" The nodded reply was enthusiastic and River had to smile. "Oh Maisie, that's fantastic! Who, when? Come on spill, I want details."

*****

They sat at the bar while Maisie related the courtship that Mambo considered sufficient, River kept grinning until Maisie mentioned War and Race. She shook her head when Maisie asked her, "Have you been to the clubhouse yet?"

"No, I rolled in and this was my first stop. I wondered how it worked out for you the morning I left, but you were smiling and hanging onto each other, looking happy. I've been hoping that everything worked out well between you. I can see that it must have." She patted the small tummy bump. "I love it. You'll make a great momma."

The peaceful smile on the smaller woman's face said it all as far as River was concerned. She was finally happy and her life turned out better than she'd ever dreamed it would.

River looked at the time and decided that she might as well bite the bullet and go to the clubhouse. That was the plan until Maisie told her, "Race and War got into a fight at the strip club over in Madison two days ago. They are sitting in jail waiting for the charges to be dropped or the prosecutor to try to cut them a deal. The dumb bastard has no idea who he's dealing with." She shrugged her shoulder and grinned. "He's gonna find out, because I heard Mambo talking to Bam last night. They are trying to find the books that Wolfman had with the payouts in them. He had the entire judicial branch of the county on the payroll. When Wolfy died, the payoffs dried up. Now if they can find the books, Mr. Prosecutor is going down the hard way, or he'll tuck his tail between his legs and skedaddle back to his office. From what Mambo said, they are in a safe place, but they rechecked the bunkers and didn't find anything. They think they might be in a locker at the bus station or a bank safety deposit box, but no one knows the combination or has any way to get the information."

River said her goodbyes and left the bar to take a room at the old No Tell Motel for the night. At midnight she sat bolt upright in the bed and gasped. That's it, those were the numbers Tuck told her about. She dug through the pockets of the leather jacket that had belonged to Dallas, and found the notebook that she'd written everything Tuck had told her to keep notes on.

She remembered him laughing and saying that, "I have the bastard by the short hairs and the dumb fucker doesn't know it yet. I've got his shit, and he ain't getting it back, so keep the numbers close. I might need you to retrieve some things for me in a few months."

She couldn't sleep and got up to pace for a while, but ended up grabbing her bag and helmet. Busses ran twenty four seven, so the station should be open for her to look for the locker.

The place was run down and there were two winos lying against each other on a bench near the bathrooms. The desk clerk was snoozing in his chair, and it was obvious that the place saw little or no nighttime traffic. The first locker number that she had, didn't match up with anything in the place, so she worked her way through the list of numbers until she found number eighty four. She punched in the combination of numbers and the door cracked open so she could push it further open to see inside. A large duffel was stuffed into the small space, but she didn't bother to open it right then. The drunks were waking up and one started to yell at the other one for finishing the bottle off without sharing.

She pulled the duffle closer to her body and shut the locker after making sure that it was empty. On the way back to the motel, she speculated about what was in the heavy bag.

She'd been expecting a book with numbers, but when she opened the thing and saw the bundles of cash, she had to sit down quick or fall down in shock. Once she'd come to terms that there was more cash in the bag than she'd ever seen in one spot outside of television, she dumped the thing on the bed and began to count the bundles of hundreds and twenties. There was over a hundred thousand dollars in the bag, and a key with a small tag that she had to take over to the light from the lamp in the room to see what was written on it. All it had was an address two towns' over. She repacked the bag, and knew that she was going to continue her search for the missing books. She needed to sleep, and sometime just before dawn she drifted off.

It was ten in the morning when she woke up and decided what to do with the bag full of money. She couldn't leave it in the motel, no one with any brains would leave anything of value in the place. Deciding to take a chance, she rode up to the gate at the Winery, and yelled at the sleepy looking prospect. "Make sure this gets put in Race's room and don't get sticky fingered. I know how much is in it and I promise you, you don't want to face the man if any of its missing."

She saw Bam heading towards the gate and pointed his way. "Give it to him, that way you won't get into trouble." She revved the sporty and left as fast as she dared to go in the curves. Her next stop was Dannefel and she still needed to eat something and gas up before trying to find the house or building where the key belonged. The town was a little smaller than Braxton Hills, but she was in unfamiliar territory.

The small house was on a cul-de-sac at the end of a dead end street with five houses scattered between the unkempt woods and wild weeds. The place looked abandoned, and two windows had been shot out with possibly a BB gun or rocks. There were two tax sale notices on the door, and disconnect tags from the utility companies. The weed yard appeared to be almost as high as the rest of the houses she'd passed on the drive into the road.

She shut the sporty down and looked around before dismounting. No one was around, in fact the only living, breathing beings was the raccoon waddling across the driveway and the birds chirping at her for intruding on their quiet spot. She reached for her pistol and thumbed the safety off before walking around the outside of the deserted bungalow.

The small garage behind the house was locked up tight, she tried the keys, but neither one worked in the lock. She went to the back door and it easily opened when she inserted the key in the deadbolt. She pushed the door open and waited for a minute trying to listen for any movement or voices.

"Hello, is anyone home? Knock, knock." No one answered her call. She kept the gun in front of her body and walked through the house. It was a neat, little house with two bedrooms, a kitchen dining room crammed together, a smallish living room and one and a half bathrooms. The place was tidy but dusty, the furniture was limited to a double bed in the larger bedroom with the attached half bath and a few articles of clothing hung in the closet. If the unmade bed hadn't looked like someone had rolled out of it without straightening the covers, she might have walked past the dusty thing. She picked up the pillow. If his aftershave had scented the pillow, it had long since dissipated. Tears were falling as she touched the black and blue colored t-shirts that were left hanging on their plastic hangers that had obviously just been bought as the tags still remained on the clothing and that disturbed her. There was nothing personal in the room for her to hold as being Tuck's.

She abandoned the room and headed for the kitchen that had a small table and two chairs sitting by themselves in the dining area. She was afraid to look in the fridge, but cracked it open and saw that it was empty. Even the freezer contained nothing. The old six pack of longnecks sat on the counter, but they weren't the brand that Tuck used to drink at the bar. The cupboards were empty and even the drawers held nothing but a few small hand tools that she picked up and looked at. Under the sink was a few cleaning products, but the place appeared to be just a house, there was nothing here to indicate that Tuck had lived here or even visited except the clothes in the closet.

She wandered around checking in possible spots that would give her a clue for whatever she needed to find. Obviously there was something here, or the keys would not have been in the bag with all of that money. All she had to do was forget sentiment and start being methodical about her search.

She was filthy and sweating by the time she found the old book that she'd almost tossed into the trash. The inside of the book was gone, but the key in the middle of the hole cut into the pages yielded another clue, and she wanted to smack Tuck for his paranoia. The damned book was under the bed with several skin magazines and an ashtray filled with butts.

She walked outside to the garage and used the key in the service door to open it up. "Oh fuck, brother, what were you doing here?"

There was a shrouded car of some sort, and a bike that was painted yellow and flamed in pussy pink. It was a Heritage softail and she envied the person that actually owned the bike. She couldn't resist sitting on the leather seat and gripping the handlebars. This bike would fit her perfectly, the original owner must have been short like her. It had certainly been well taken care of because the only thing she could see to complain about was the dust covering the beautiful machine.

She got off the bike with a final sigh and began exploring in the limited lighting. Remembering what she had to do to find the key to the garage, she started in the corner of the building and began to look and touch ever inch of the walls and cabinets. She found the name Tuck on a few of the tools and knew that she was onto something there. At last she had proof that Tuck was there, and more than likely he'd been moving in, just before he was murdered by that bastard Wolfman.

In the top drawer she found something that damn near killed her. It was a birthday card, addressed to *"the best little sister a man could have."*

"Dear River, I've been busy, but I hope you like the softail, I painted it all girly because I've been thinking that you should drop the Dyke thing. You are beautiful and unless your tastes have changed drastically, it's time for you to be yourself. I'll be

home by Christmas, and I hope you let your hair grow out and can paint some makeup on that pretty face so I can take you out on the town and show you off. I'll have to fight the scum from coming on to you, but maybe you can find a decent man that will love you like you deserve to be loved.

Dallas tells me that you are restless but hanging in there with him while you wait for me to come home. I'm ready to settle down and grow old, maybe find an ole' lady and have a few crumb crunchers crawling around. I'm not getting any younger, you know. I'm just a few weeks from accomplishing my goal of bringing that bastard down. Once I do that, I'm hanging the colors up, and joining you and Dallas there. Most of the brothers are great guys, but there are others that need a noose. Oh well, I'll have plenty of time to tell my stories over and over like Dallas does, so you are warned.

BTW, I learned how to use a computer, you were wrong, my damned head isn't too thick to learn stuff. Love you kiddo, Tuck

She folded the card and put it back into the envelope, and slid it into the top of her boot. She wiped the tears away with a grubby hand and continued her search.

It took her three hours to move things out and around the small space, but she'd finally found the thumb drive. It was stuck in a jar of nuts and bolts, and she wanted to wring Tuck's neck yet again. She was greasy and filthy from head to toe, but she would have the answers and now that she looked at the softail, she would be taking possession of it in the very near future.

She locked the house and garage just before sunset, heading back to the motel to clean up.

The Tech Store was closed by the time she scrubbed the day's filth from her body, and she settled for dinner at the local Truck Stop up by the highway. They had good food, homemade mashed potatoes and gravy coupled with deep fried fish and a nice, big slice of blueberry pie made her feel much better. For some reason the food gave her a little shot of happy, and she smiled at the cashier on her way out of the door.

Sleep was hard to find even though the bed was comfortable and the sheets were clean. She dreamed of War and his lips exploring her body. Then Race and his almost scary form of arousing her body made her groan in the darkness. She wanted those two like she wanted to breathe, but they had to come to terms and for once they wouldn't get the last words.

CHAPTER 19

The cell door opened and the deputy stood with his hand on his belt close to the Taser that the dumbass carried. Race had been in solitary for almost two weeks, the Judge had refused to grant bail because he was considered a flight risk. Four times the Prosecutor himself had visited and wanted to know if Race had anything he wanted to tell him, and four times the man had left with a red face and a hard case of mad. He kept threatening to 'throw the book at you,' and 'bury you under the jail.'

Race knew what the fucker was angling for, but he'd be damned if he was going to pay the son-of-a-bitch off. Or worse, be charged with bribing a court official. The original charges were petty bullshit, and according to the MC's suits, they were ready for a court date to chew the Prosecutor into bits.

Now he was being escorted to the front desk. The smug bastard behind the desk handed him an envelope with his personal possessions inside, and Race checked everything for signs of tampering. All of his cards, licenses, and pictures had been stuffed back into the wallet, and he glared at the fat cop.

"I see that you searched my things, you invaded my property and privacy, and there's two hundred dollars missing from my wallet. I want my lawyer to be here, and I want you to tell him what happened to my money. And where's my fuckin' phone? God damned thieving cops anyway."

He tensed when someone came up beside him and reached for the envelope with the rest of his possessions. His watch, three gold rings, a small hoop earring, were dumped on the counter with his smart phone that had the screen smashed and looked totaled. Race scowled when he saw River standing there.

"What in the hell are you doing here, where's War and the suits?" He cut his eyes toward the now red faced cop. "If you fuckers took my goddamned bike and there's a scratch on it, someone will be paying."

River took his arm and handed him the envelope. "Here, put your things back into the envelope and let's go. You can file a complaint. Come on tough guy, move it."

The cop cleared his throat and opened his mouth, but she shut him up with a look and the comment 'this fine upstanding officer of the law' has a date that should be here any time now. War is coming down the hall and as soon as he gets his stuff, we'll leave quietly and peacefully, you get me?"

Race nodded his head, but still shot the fucker at the desk a nasty look that promised retribution. The deputy that had escorted Race from his cell had vanished, but War's escort was walking three paces behind the big man and he had his hand on the butt of his Glock.

War looked like a wild man, his hair was a mess, and the two-week old beard was raggedy to say the least. He didn't look right or left, he walked up to the desk and snarled at the cop. When the deputy removed the cuffs from his wrists, he stepped back quickly assuming his hand to gun pose.

"Tell this dumb fuck to get his hand off of the gun, or does he plan to shoot me in the back, like the rest of you cowardly fuckers would?"

The desk cop looked at the wary deputy and shook his head, but he turned back to War and told him to "shut the fuck up, asshole."

River walked towards him slowly and angled herself in beside him, saying, "Hey, you look like hell, but I decided to take you home." The look he shot her made her smile. Yeah, he was happy to see her, but right at the moment he was pissed beyond normal.

"I've got Race here too, so look at your stuff quick, it'll be dark soon, and I'm tired from all the running I've been doing for the two of you. Hurry up, let's go."

The expensive watch he'd won in a poker game was missing and his necklace had been snapped. As with Race, money was missing from his wallet, his phone was smashed too, and they'd shoved his stuff back into the wallet. "Bunch of thieves, rotten motherfuckers."

She was getting tired of listening to the shit about cops being everything from motherfuckers to pedophiles, and so she pinched War on the ass to get his attention.

"Look, I'm tired. I'm ready to take you home, but so help me if the two of you don't shut it and get moving I'll leave your asses here. *Let's go.*"

She was the first one out the door and by that time she was beginning to regret springing their asses from jail. It hadn't taken much to convince the prosecutor to drop his charges and allow the men to walk free. At least not after she handed one of the photo screen shots from the thumb drive she'd found at Tuck's place. It was a record of bribe money paid to the man's account via wire transfers, and he'd paled right there in the hallway when she gave it to him on his way to court.

"I suggest that you reconsider the extortion attempt that you are trying to get from the bikers. I can only imagine what might happen if the originals ended up at the capitol on a certain desk or two."

Now they were free, and she was not about to deal with their bullshit. The worry about them was over, and she still had things to do before she would be ready to deal with their crap.

Mambo was pulling into the parking lot just as she mounted her yellow bike and she waved as she started the engine and snugged the helmet onto her head. He was driving the club's support vehicle to pick up War and Race. Their bikes had been taken back to the clubhouse the night that they had been arrested before the cops could confiscate them, so Race's rant had been for nothing, but the bikes had been saved from destruction at the hands of the uncaring tow truck drivers.

She heard the shouts from the men as she revved the softail, but chose to ignore them, and pulled from the lot. She knew she would return to the winery, but not until she finished her own business. Once she dealt with her brother's business, she would be free to deal with her own future.

*****

War was still telling the cop what he thought of police in general and the man behind the desk looked like he wanted to be anywhere but in front of the big biker towering over him, when River had slipped out of the door, and Race put his hand on War's shoulder to get his attention.

"Come on man, like she said, we'll file a report. It won't do much good, but that's what happens when people stop getting juice money, they want that income, so they steal it."

War snarled at the cop again and grabbed his shit from the table. He continued to mumble about "lowlife fuckers" even as they walked into the late afternoon sunshine.

They saw River sitting on a bright yellow softail and when she appeared to be leaving without talking to them, they yelled at her to wait up. She kept on riding, and that pissed them off.

"What the fuck, she gets us out, and takes off. Oh I'm gonna bust her ass when I get my hands on her." Race stomped down the steps even as War had already made it to the bottom stair. "I'm gonna tie her little ass to the bed and after I'm done spanking her I'm gonna fuck her until she can't move."

War nodded in agreement as they walked towards the van. "As soon as I get a fuckin' shower and clean up, I'm going looking for her and when I get a hold on her little ass she won't be so sassy mouthed. She pinched me and told me to shut up.

What the hell is she playing at anyway? Run in, get the helpless bad asses' out of jail and disappear? She's been gone for fuckin' months and thinks she can just waltz in and run back out. She needs a lesson alright, and she'd gonna get one."

Race stopped at the door of the van and looked at Mambo accusingly. "Why didn't you stop her, and where the fuck did that softail come from? She's too little to be riding a bike like that."

Mambo grinned and shook his head as the men got in the vehicle. "Not my woman and not my business. She stopped by the bar an hour and a half ago and was conspiring with Maisie at the bar while I was changing the kegs. Next thing I know, they're out front and Maisie is oohing and ahhing over that yellow bike, and squealing because River gave her an old sporty. Said it was hers, but now she had her birthday gift from her brother, so she didn't need it."

Race looked at him in disbelief, "I thought the brother was dead, and when did she start riding anyway? She took that turn off out of here like she's been riding for years, not a few months."

Mambo shrugged his shoulders and checked the mirrors before answering. "He is dead, from what Maisie says. River has secrets, and plans to stick around, so she'll turn up eventually. It took four minutes for Maisie to start in on me to teach her to ride her scoot. Her feet even touch the ground. By the way, you should know that I'm not real happy with your woman myself right now, my ole' lady is pregnant, and she ain't learning to do shit until my kid is born."

War smacked him on the shoulder. "That's great man, congrats on the kid. You'll make a damn good father, and we can help out if you need it. I can't remember the last time we had a new generation born into the group."

Mambo grinned and laughed. "Yeah, I 'bout shit my pants when she started puking every morning. Coffee makes her blow chunks, and she can't work the kitchen at the bar anymore because the smell of frying grease sends her to the bathroom or out the back door. Maisie offered River a job, but she turned it down. She said that she had plans, so that's all I know about the woman. I've got shit to do, I don't have time to sit in on their jabbering."

Mambo dropped them at the winery and left. The first thing they saw was Bam swilling a beer and Kink wasn't looking too happy, mainly because Bam had his hand around his throat and kept him pinned to the tabletop. Elton and Joey were standing close to the table, but neither man bothered to look up when the door shut behind Race and War.

Goody watched the two men walk in and waved, but her attention was back on the drama unfolding in the room within seconds of acknowledging their presence.

Race had to strain to hear what Bam was saying to his victim.

"You wanna beat on someone motherfucker, I'm here. You can't fucking pick a fight with a man, but you damn sure like using your fists on a woman. So since my fists didn't make you understand the last time to keep your fuckin' hands to yourself, I'm gonna cut the fuckers off and see how you like that." The beer bottle in his hand smashed onto the table and the top half remained in Bam's fist. He grinned and slammed the jagged glass down into the palm of Kink's hand, causing the man to scream.

"I warned you, cocksucker, you should've listened." Bam twisted the glass in his fist that was still embedded in Kink's right hand. "You like pain don't 'cha, fucking coward. Too fuckin' bad you like to give it, 'cause by the time I'm finished, you'll be feeling it. I'd kill you, but that's up to the club, if they can find some use for you fine, make damn sure you don't come into my line of sight again or you die. Do you understand me, you crazy fuck?"

The screams stopped, but Kink was losing blood and he was starring at death in Bam's eyes. He knew his days were numbered, but the urge to watch the whore beg for her life had been too much to resist. Better to get it done and over with. "Fuck you, she begged for it, crawled on her knees and begged me to hit her, she loved it. She wore that short skirt to fuckin' tease me into it, and she fuckin' begged me." His grin was what did it, he saw Bam's eyes change from anger to intent, and he laughed even through the bloody swollen lips from Bam's fists earlier. "You pussy, she begged for it."

Bam raised the bottle neck and brought it down to drop it on the floor and fisted his hand before he began punching Kink's face. His fist kept hitting the man's nose and between his eyes, and his other hand was squeezing his windpipe to stop him from breathing.

Race didn't interfere. If he'd been in Bam's position, he'd have done the same thing. Once he was sure that the brother had accomplished his goal of putting the world out of the misery of Kink being in it, he stepped up next to the furious man.

"Hey brother, glad to see you saw to things while I was gone. We should have dealt with this piece of trash a long time ago." He slapped Bam on the shoulder and debated whether to tell him that Kink was done. "You ready to fill me in on the past two weeks? War was stinking so bad that I thought I'd have to hose his big ass off out in the yard when we got back, so he's heading to the shower. You've got time to finish your business and get something on your knuckles before he gets back. If you come lookin' for me, I'll be over at that table with a cold one waiting." He nodded in the direction of the corner table and walked away.

His distraction must have brought Bam back to his senses, because he stopped hitting his victim, and wiped his knuckles on the bloody t-shirt that declared the wearer to be "Ridin' Free." He shook his head and breathed deeply, then turned towards the bar.

Elton and Joey stepped up and carried Kink's carcass out of the room while Goody was busy with wrapping Bam's hand in an antiseptic soaked towel.

Flats sat beside Race and they made small talk until Flats told him about the strange shit happening around the club.

"First you should know that the bikes are safely tucked inside the warehouse, and Bam and me are the ones that rode them back home the night that the cops started that shit with you. We went back later and got our scoots."

Race thanked him. "Cool brother, I'd hate to have to take a new paintjob out on some tow truck driver, but I would've done it." He knew that Flats wasn't finished because of the way he kept playing with his fingers and tapping them on the table. "Okay, let's have it. I was gone almost two weeks, so I'm sure shit went on here."

Flats grimaced and nodded. "Yeah, shit went on, surprised that Bam didn't kill the fucker before now. You know how the women go around and change the towels and clean the bathrooms and shit?" Race frowned and nodded, so Flats continued.

"Well Yo-Yo caught one of the prospects trying to get into your room, and she damn near killed the dumb fucker pushing him down the stairs. Bam can tell you about that, I don't know enough to speak about it.

"There's been more deliveries from River in the past week, and since her name was on the boxes, we put them in the house out back, but the tool boxes we put in the warehouse on the end that doesn't have a leak in the roof. There's some expensive equipment out there and we didn't want it to get ruined."

Race knew that the men would value such things and he appreciated that they took the trouble to keep them dry. Flats was still holding out, so he said to the older man, "Just come out with what you want to say. I need some sleep and I know I'm not gonna get any for a while, so spill man, don't give me the hem hawing shit."

Flats tightened his lips, and then opened them enough to start talking. "I took the skin flicks back to the video store and met Georgia. She's a good looking woman and I've been seeing her for the past week now. I want to bring her here, but I thought I'd ask before waltzing her in the club, you know what I mean?"

Race was expecting more bad news, so he was relieved when Flats finally came out with his problem. He wasn't asking to bring the woman in for the weekend, he was wanting to bring her in as his woman. "We need a policy about citizens, but for now, bring her in on the weekend and let the club get to know her before we start thinking access permission. She's a good sort, so give her a chance to make an impression."

Flats nodded and looked relieved. Race had to sympathize with the brother, after all, women were the devil to deal with and drove many a good man to drink and do shit like getting locked down with her pussy being the only one a man was allowed to have as long as they were together. Thinking about how Shorty had put a lock on his dick already just depressed him.

War came down the stairs and Flats excused himself to send Goody over with drinks. He was anxious to call Georgia and invite her to the club this weekend.

War sat down and kicked his feet up on the table. Bam finally walked over and sat down, knocking War's booted feet from the tabletop.

"I get enough crap from these fuckers, I don't want your shit kickers in my face while I relax." He took one of the longnecks from Goody's hand as she walked up to deposit her tray of drinks in front of the men. "Thanks."

War asked what had been happening lately. "I've been locked up in a fucking cage for days without seeing sunshine and I'm edgy, so tell me something good to take my mind off of the place."

Bam decided to lay it out. "You want the full story, here it is. Your woman dropped a bag full of cash off at the gate and told the prospect not to steal any of it, she knew how much was there, she saw me, told him to avoid temptation and just give it to me." He shook his head and looked at the two men in front of him. "There's a hundred large in that fuckin' bag, I put it in your closet. The boy decided that he might like to lift a few bucks, even though he didn't know how much was in the bag. Long story short, Yo-Yo found him hiding in your bathroom, she kicked his ass down the stairs and told me what he'd been doing. Nobody knows about the cash but him and me, and he's not doing a lot of talking right now." He grinned. "I gave him to Queenie to play with, and the last I knew, he was hanging in the shed where she likes to play."

War laughed and clapped his hands. "Now that's a well deserved punishment for trying to steal from a brother if I ever heard of one. Fuck me, but she's an evil bitch when she gets in the mood. Did you see what she did to that little wanna be that kept coming around trying to play the biker? He was a whipped puppy that she pulled around on a leash until the bitch got tired of him and swatted his ass at the gate to make him leave."

Race wondered aloud, "Where in the hell did Shorty get that kind of scratch?"

Bam shrugged. "Hell man, I got no idea about that. The boxes of shit that keep showing up at the gate are a pain in the ass. Some days there's one, two days later, three show up. I just decided to shove 'em in the house and let you all sort it out." He thought about that day's delivery, and got up to walk over to the bar and pulled a large manila envelope from the shelf before bringing it back and handing it to Race.

"That came today." He sat back and took a long pull on his beer while Race frowned at the thing in his hand. "It ain't gonna bite you, I carried it from the front gate into the building this morning."

War reached over and took the thick envelope from Race's hand and ripped open the seal. He looked at the contents, and shook his head before reaching inside and pulling a plastic bound booklet out and tossing it towards Race. "There you go, no anthrax or powdery shit, you can rest easy."

The booklet read like a who's who of people that had taken payoffs from Wolfman and the Breed over the past decade. The totals were staggering, and until he saw the prosecutor's name and that of his predecessor, Race hadn't fully comprehended what River had done to get them released from jail.

He shoved the thing back towards War and considered what he'd read. The Breed had paid thousands to keep the authorities off their backs for years. Now they needed to decide what to do with the information. This was going to take some time and thought before they took any kind of action.

Bam was next to read the booklet and he tossed it back to Race. "I wondered how she got you out of there, what's the bet that she leaned on Bernie, the pompous asshole, to spring you?"

They knew that he was referring to Bernard Landers, also known as Attorney Landers, the Prosecutor for the county. According to the bank statements they'd just read, good old Bernie had received well over ten grand a year from Wolfman until his death.

"No bet, our girl has been a busy bee, and I plan to clip her wings. She shows up again, I don't care where, I want to know about it."

CHAPTER 20

It had taken her another week to square away Tuck's secret life, and it still surprised her to see the portfolio that her brother had invested his money wisely. She was now a very wealthy woman, in fact she owned every house or held the note on every house on the road where she'd found the answers that she came looking for. Not to mention several other properties that were leased to businesses in three towns.

Her legal name had been listed with his as owner of record on all of the properties and she wondered if Tuck knew that his days were numbered, because she found small notes on the list of properties she'd found in one of the tool boxes in the garage. He explained why he bought each property and his vision for each of them. The money from his share of their parents' estate had seeded his investments, and she had no idea that her brother was so smart. He'd planned on selling everything in a year or so and being long gone from the town and the Breed.

Now it was time for her to talk with Race and War. It had been months since they'd been intimate, they had probably forgotten about it, but she hadn't gone a day without thinking about the way they looked, talked, and the fantastic way she'd felt between them.

After talking to Maisie, who had her information from Mambo, War and Race had issued a standing order to find her and follow her, and report it to them immediately. It gave her hope, so she had begun having her things sent to the winery for safekeeping. After all, they already had most of her belongings, so what would make the difference if she put everything in one place? If the men were still interested, she wanted to explore the possibility of a relationship. It would be awkward at first, but they might make it work. If they were not interested, then she had a nice little house right here, and time to decide what to do with her life.

She took the time to do her nails and used the make-up kit that she bought two years before, and stood back from the mirror to assess the result of her primping. She shrugged her shoulders and decided that this was as good as she could do, so it was time to stop dragging her feet and get it in gear.

There was yet another prospect at the gate, and she saw that he was an older guy than the pimply faced one from the last time she'd stopped there to hand over the bag of money. This one had his cell in hand as soon as she idled in front of the gate, and he wasted no time opening it for her to ride through. He nodded and went back to his business.

She rode up to the front of the winery and parked her bike, taking the time to fluff her hair after removing the helmet and setting it on the seat of the bike. She took a couple deep breaths and headed for the open door.

Goody was behind the bar and her eyes widened when she saw River walk in. She grinned and started to come around the bar to greet her, but stopped when she saw Race coming up behind her fast. War was coming in the room from the hallway and he grabbed her arm, stopping her from walking further into the room. Race was still three paces behind River, he nodded as War picked her up and tossed her over his shoulder. Race turned back to the door and War followed with River hanging upside down.

"You can let me down; I'm not going to run." He didn't bother to answer, he just kept walking. "You should know I came here to talk with you guys, to see if maybe we could get together, you know, like communicate? I can walk you know, my legs aren't broken."

She got a heavy hand on the right cheek of her ass for her trouble of trying to reason with the big oaf. She yanked his shoulder length hair and pushed herself up, but he grunted and smacked her ass again. His gruff, "Knock it off," made her eyes narrow. She kept her handful of his hair and tensed to try to overbalance him, but he stopped in his tracks in front of an old wooden door while Race reached around and opened the thing.

She could see hardwood floors, and a few pieces of new looking furniture, but the hands pulling her boots from her feet made her kick her legs, getting yet another slap on her ass. War's hands held her thighs up from his body and she thought he was going to put her down, but she felt fingers working the fastening on her jeans and moving to the sides of the material to peel them off, taking her French cut panties with them. Feeling the wetness of the crotch of her underwear sliding down her thighs embarrassed her, and she reached down to War's side and pinched his skin to distract him when the two men started talking about her token resistance.

Him saying, "Just stop resisting, we can see and feel how much you want this too," was what got him the pinch. Her retaliation is what got her several smacks on her ass and she screamed more for their benefit than from pain.

Fingers trailing from the small of her back into the crease of her ass and down to her clit made her squirm, but War held her steady and when he licked the skin on her side closest to his face, she giggled. She tried to keep it in, but his whiskers tickled her sensitive nerves, and instead of letting her go, his lips sucked the spot as he turned his head slightly from side to side, worrying the skin and making her squeal. She levered herself up with both hands planted on his hips, saw Race's chest and looking down, she could see that he was in no condition to be reasonable. He didn't have a stitch of clothing on, and her mouth watered at the sight of his bare flesh.

Her hands abandoned War's hips and reached for the thickly muscled chest in front of her, but he was pulling her shirt from her back and unsnapping the back of her bra so it would fall with the shirt. He left the material around her head and upper arms, while his fingers tortured her nipples and she groaned in frustration.

War was trailing his fingers through her slit and dipping them into her drenched pussy, still kissing and licking the skin of her side and hip. Race was talking, but it took more concentration than she possessed at the moment to register what he was saying until he twisted her nipples and told her to listen up.

"You've been a bad girl, and we've been kept away from you long enough. I don't know why you took off like that, but the next time you decide to sneak out of here, I'll track you down and do more than just give you the spanking that I'm about to give you. We've been worried sick and you couldn't be bothered to answer your damn phone, let alone send a fuckin' postcard."

She could hear the hurt under the anger in his voice, and even though she thought that she had a good reason to leave at the time, she felt ashamed for sneaking out like that. "I'm sorry."

It was the only thing she got to say before she was tossed onto a big bed and Race came down over her, kissing her lips and sliding his cock into her pussy while she moved her hips trying to adjust to his thickness penetrating her small entrance. Every time she tried to speak, his lips took hers and his tongue licked at hers, sliding along side, up and around. She was breathless when he broke the kiss and groaned against the tender skin of her neck.

"I owe you a spanking, but right this minute, I need to be inside you. So shut up, and pretend that your pussy isn't soaking my cock, and clamping down trying to keep it when I back out." On his fourth stroke, he buried his cock as far as he could go, and reached down to slide his hand under her waist, before rolling them over with her seated completely on his hips and his cock was kissing her cervix. "Fuck yes, this is where you belong, so damned tight it feels like your squeezing my cock. Ride me Shorty, you can take over for a bit."

She was as full as she'd ever been, even when War had been buried as deep as Race now was. Feeling fingers sliding between the cheeks of her ass, poking gently at her asshole made her tense up and Race groan from her tightening, trying to keep the intruder from the small hole that War was pushing his thick finger into.

War grabbed a handful of her hair and pulled her head back so he could kiss her and once her mouth was opened under his, he pushed his finger deep inside the tightest spot it had ever been inside of. He left the finger there while she moaned into his mouth and her muscles relaxed around his sliding finger as it began fucking her ass. Her body quivered, he could feel the way her inner muscles began to clamp and release as an orgasm took over her body and she began to jerk around, screaming between her teeth. He was lucky that he'd pulled his tongue back, or she'd have bitten it in two when her jaws clenched shut like that. He slid a second finger deep and she jerked again, while her body clamped down on his fingers. He pumped his lubed fingers a few more times and knew that if he didn't sink his dick in soon, he'd be shooting his cum over her back like some snot nosed teen that had no control.

He gave her hair another pull, and held the cheek of her ass with one hand to slide his cock into her asshole. "Race, pull back a bit if you can, I need some space for a second." He felt the thickness receding and slid the head of his cock past her sphincter, feeling the heat and tightness of her asshole clamp down on his dick. "Fuck me, so tight, so damn tight." He had to take a few breaths to slow himself down, and not slam his cock deep in a single stroke. She was squirming as it was and he didn't want to hurt her, but when she backed her ass up and pushed down on him, he groaned and rested his head between her shoulder blades.

She wasn't thinking, all she was doing was feeling, and she wanted more of that bite and kiss. The thickness in her ass sent nibbles of pain and pleasure at the same time, but the cock in her pussy was pure pleasure. She reached her hand up and grabbed War's shoulder, but her hand slid off of his damp skin. She grabbed a handful of his hair with one hand and sank her nails into the lightly furred chest under the hand she used to balance her body. Then she began moving on the men that enticed her into being someone that didn't think, only felt, and it didn't seem that she would ever get enough of this unrelenting need and pleasure.

"Love, oh god, this...more." Those were her only words as she moved her hips, not realizing that the men were allowing her to take what she needed and enjoying the sight and knowledge that she wanted them as much as they needed her. She felt her mind go bright white and the colors burst in her brain as she screamed while her orgasm shoved everything but pleasure from her body and brain. She was strung tight one second, boneless the next, needing to constantly move her hips for those tiny aftershocks that made her shiver. She grabbed her breasts, pulling her own nipples from her body and crying out while the pleasure continued to flow through her. She'd felt the warm liquid flowing into her from the men, but the slickness only enhanced her pleasure and she was crying before she collapsed onto Race's chest. She felt War's cock withdrawing slowly and Race's cock was softening, but she couldn't move from her claimed spot on top of Race. She didn't want to move, she didn't want to talk, all she wanted was to lie there and enjoy the small shocks of pleasured nerve endings deep inside.

War got up and went into the bathroom. On his way back, he stopped at the dresser and opened the top drawer, withdrawing a small leather pouch. He came back to the bed, opening the drawstring, dropping the rings that he and Race had bought all those long months ago. Race nodded his head and War handed him one of the rings before pulling her left hand towards him.

She turned her head to see what he was doing, never expecting him to slide a gold band on her finger. When he raised her hand to his lips and kissed the ring and her knuckles, she choked up, but when Race mimicked his actions with a ring of his own, she lost it. She held both of their hands and squeezed tight as she tried without success to tell them how much they meant to her.

She hated blubbering like a baby, but she couldn't stop it, and Race held her tight to his chest telling her, "We'll work it out, whatever we need to do to make you happy, we'll find a way."

War rubbed her lower back and kissed her shoulder. "I still owe you a spanking, but that can wait. Race is right, we'll work it out. I've wanted you since I saw you strutting around the bar with a tray full of drinks and that sassy smile on your lips. The feeling didn't go away, and you've become an obsession for me, one that I have no intention of letting go."

Race rolled them to their sides, and her legs didn't want to straighten out from their crouched position, she laughed, but couldn't believe that these two sexy assed, bad boys wanted to commit to her. She loved them, she'd known it almost from the start, but they needed to know and they needed to hear what she needed besides amazing, mind blowing sex. She finally sat up on her own and patted the bed on each side of her indicating that she wanted them to sit and talk. Race groaned, but complied and War shook his head and plopped down too.

She starred at the rings on her finger, and marveled that they had the things waiting for her. She looked at each man and smiled through her red eyes and tearstained cheeks. "I left because I didn't want to be a passaround when you got tired of me. I'm not wired like that. I missed you guys so much, you have no idea, but I took care of my unfinished business. I gave myself time to grieve for my brother and Dallas, and I finally learned to like myself. Sometime I'll have to tell you about the past few months, but you should know that there wasn't a day that went by that I didn't think about the two of you."

She fiddled with the rings and took a deep breath before telling them, "I love you guys, and it's been hell being without you. I didn't realize it until I'd been gone for a few days, and by then I knew I had to deal with my personal issues before I could get involved any deeper with you." She looked from one man to the other. "I hope that makes sense to you because that's the only way I know how to tell you that I love you and I'm whole now, all of the loose ends are taken care of in my life, so I'm able to give you my all."

She shivered when War's bearded cheek brushed hers and he said, "I love you too, but you are still getting that spanking I promised you later."

Race nuzzled the other side of her neck and said, "We bought the rings the day you left. We stopped at the jewelers and picked them up because we knew that you were the one for us. When we got here and you were gone, it tore me up. Don't ever do that again. I've never loved a woman before and it felt like my guts were torn out and layin' on the floor. For the record, I love you too."

Race stood up and stretched his big body, which drew her eyes, and she licked her lips, but he shook his head. "Not right yet Shorty, you need to soak in a hot tub of water for a while and we need to scare up some eats. With you around, I'm gonna need food so I'm not too weak to satisfy you." He dodged the pillow that she threw, and War shook his head at them.

"I'll be right back and we can decide what you want for dinner."

He headed for the bathroom and River hugged the other pillow to her chest as she watched War put his clothes on. Life with the two of them would be interesting, and she couldn't wait for later, she grabbed War by the hips and yanked him down beside her on the bed.

*****

Bam watched Yo-Yo as she walked across the floor toward the bar, and considered asking her to bed down with him for the night. She fascinated him, and the few times that he'd enjoyed having sex with her had been memorable. She hadn't balked at anything he wanted to do with her or to her, but she still refused to discuss her past. She told him that she'd share her body with him, but her life belonged to her, and no one was entitled to her memories but her. He didn't push her, after all, everyone had secrets and a past, even he did. She was a beautiful woman and the more he was around her, the more he wanted her. He stood up and headed her way.

ABOUT THE AUTHOR

RYDER DANE

I write about MC Groups aka Biker Books, because I've lived with Motorcycles my entire life. It made me smile when a reviewing reader said that there was a realistic feel to my writing! Having been an "Old Lady" since I was 19 gives me the advantage of using a few real details of MC life. I am very happy to bring readers my stories and having them invest in my characters' lives.

Website: <u>Ryderdane.com</u>

Books by Ryder Dane
Big Dog (Burning Bastards MC Book 1)
Nomad's Fall (Burning Bastards MC Book 2)
Charlie's Heart
(Burning Bastards MC Series Book 3)

Sanctuary Within the Breed
(Lucifer's Breed MC Book 1)
Integrity Has No Bounds
(Lucifer's Breed MC Book 2)
Starting Over (Lucifer's Breed MC Book 3)